I surface from my dream with a yell, realize where I am, and clamp my hands over my mouth. I'm not buried under tons of water, I'm not even in the ambulance with Aunt Grace and my mother — I'm in bed in Lavner Bay, Oregon, in the business which my aunt left me. After she drowned. I sit up and hug my knees, a horrible realization coming over me. Unless things had changed drastically for Grace — some heavy-duty therapy for her fear of water and some swimming lessons — the likelihood of her having drowned while snorkeling was nil. Oh she drowned all right — I believed that — but what was she doing in the water? Water which, the last time I knew about it, she feared? I pull the blankets up around my chin, realizing that I'm way, way out of my depth. And then, because the image is so bizarre, I start to laugh, but the laughter quickly turns to tears. Help, I call silently, drawing the blankets protectively up to my chin. I need help.

Death at Lavender Bay

AN ALLISON O'NEIL MYSTERY

LAUREN WRIGHT DOUGLAS

THE NAIAD PRESS, INC.
1996

Printed in the United States of America on acid-free paper
First Edition

Edited by Christine Cassidy
Cover design by Bonnie Liss (Phoenix Graphics)
Typeset by Sandi Stancil

Library of Congress Cataloging-in-Publication Data

Douglas, Lauren Wright, 1947–
    Death at Lavender Bay : an Allison O'Neil mystery / by Lauren
Wright Douglas.
        p.   cm.
    ISBN 1-56280-085-X
    I. Title.
PS3554.O8263D4   1996
813'.54—dc20
                                                            96-23002
                                                            CIP

For Martha, as always

Books by Lauren Wright Douglas

DEATH AT LAVENDER BAY
(An Allison O'Neil Mystery)

CAITLIN REECE MYSTERIES
THE ALWAYS ANONYMOUS BEAST
NINTH LIFE
THE DAUGHTERS OF ARTEMIS
A TIGER'S HEART
GOBLIN MARKET
A RAGE OF MAIDENS

As Zenobia N. Vole:
OSTEN'S BAY

About the Author

Lauren Wright Douglas was born in Canada in 1947. She grew up in a military family and spent part of her childhood in Europe. Lauren moved from Oak Bay, British Columbia, to the Southwest some years ago, but the lure of the ocean drew her westward again. She now writes on the Oregon coast, where she lives with her partner and an assortment of cats. Lauren's second novel, *Ninth Life* — a book in the Caitlin Reece series — won the 1990 Lambda Award for Best Lesbian Mystery. She is presently at work on *Cat Dancing*, the seventh Caitlin Reece novel, which will be published by Naiad late in 1997. Another Allison O'Neil novel is planned for 1997 as well.

Chapter 1

So here I am, sitting in the office of this attorney, in Salmon Armpit, Oregon (or some such unsavory place), and she tells me the most amazing thing. I, who have never owned anything of any importance except a used car, a few books that represent the inventory of my mail-order fantasy and mystery business, and my cat Sam Spade (who really owns me), now own a Bed and Breakfast on the Oregon coast. Real estate, I believe it's called. How ironic — does this mean that I, myself, am now real?

What an unsettling prospect for one who has so successfully run from reality for so long.

It seems that my elderly aunt Grace, whom I do no more than receive the occasional letter or Christmas card, drowned last week while swimming in Lavner Bay and left her B & B to *moi*, Allison O'Neil, her only niece. Whoa, I want to tell the attorney (who bears an unnerving resemblance to Barbara Bush), stop, hold on here, this is all very nice I'm sure, but I'm a California Girl, and besides *that* I have absolutely no desire to own a B & B in Oregon where it rains 283 days out of 365. I checked. Not that I'm a devotee of the sun — we're all mindful of melanomas these days — but so much rain and fog is bound to get a bit old after a while. Lavner Bay has a population of a mere 625 souls for a reason, right? So I'm trying to tell the Barbara Bush look-alike sitting across the desk from me that whereas I'm grateful that auntie cared enough to leave me her B & B, I really don't *want* it and she's telling me that it doesn't matter if I want it or not because I've got it.

"So now what?" I ask her and she fires off a give-me-strength look and heaves a sigh, just to make certain I've registered her displeasure.

"So this," she says, handing me a sheaf of papers and a handful of keys. "I need you to sign these, Miss O'Neil."

I ignore her sigh and dirty looks and tap my fingers on her desk, looking over the papers she gives me. It seems that whether or not I sign the papers, I am now the legal owner of Lavner Bay B & B so what the hell, I go ahead and sign. And then I get IT — an idea, a true inspiration, one so outrageous that it makes me smile for the first time since I've set foot in this benighted state. In fact, I'm almost giggling. I hand the papers back to Barbara and give her the benefit of a truly megawatt smile. She looks at me suspiciously.

"Copies," she says, obviously disconcerted. "I'll get you some copies of these and then you can be on your way."

I really can't wait. Looking out the window at the impossibly blue sky, the indigo ocean, and the trees that are at least a dozen shades of green, I laugh. I'm not even tempted. This is plainly one of the 82 days a year when the sun shines, trapping tourists into addle-brained fantasies of Moving to the Coast and recent heiresses into deluded dreams of Making It in Oregon. But not me. Nope, I'm not staying. I have other plans for Lavner Bay.

When the attorney comes back and hands me my copies and my keys, I tell her thanks and in a flash, I'm outta there.

The B & B isn't hard to find — everything in Lavner Bay is just down or up the road from everything else. I feel so good I'm whistling "Your Kiss Is on My List" as I wheel out of town, looking for the white two-story on the cliffs that the blonde lass at the Texaco station swore I couldn't miss. After about three miles of driving, however, I realize that indeed I must have missed it, so I turn back, proceeding so slowly that campersful of tourists and pickupsful of locals speed around me honking, some giving me the finger. I wave gaily at them (hey, I'm an heiress — I can afford a little magnanimity of spirit) and finally pull my rented Ford Escort onto the shoulder of the road, feeling a little exasperated. Because there's nothing even faintly resembling a white two-story edifice on the west side of the highway.

Deciding to leave my car where it is, I scoot across Highway 101, intending to ask directions at an imposing gray hostelry overdressed with gables and eaves and more gingerbread than a bakery. The place is set back a little from the road and I see that I'll have to walk down a little cedar-shaded lane that rambles beside it and, I hope, eventually up to the front door of the hotel. As I pass into the shade of the pines or cedars or firs or whatever, I simultaneously lose the sight of the hotel and the sounds of cars buzzing up and down 101. It's suddenly . . . very still. I look around, amazed that anything this close to the road can be so quiet. Must be the trees. I yawn, realizing just how stressful my meeting with Barbara Bush was. Well, this walk will be good for me — I'm unwinding already. On my right is a break in the cedars and a sign TO THE GARDENS and I decide what the hell, I'll take a shortcut through the flowers. The attorney mentioned that the place has an espresso bar. Maybe I can flag down a serving wench and order an iced latte. So I'm feeling pretty good, humming "In an English Country Garden" when I step through the break in the cedars.

"Holy shit," I say, breaking my New Year's resolution regarding foul language. But the occasion calls for something more than: "Cool!" Against a backdrop of postcard-pretty blue sky and indigo sea, the hotel sits at the top of a gentle slope, looking

4

like, well, like something out of an Impressionist painting. Flowers like bolts and bolts of floral printed fabric seem to spill down the slope toward me — spiky-petaled flowers the size of dinner plates in every color of the artist's palette. Small, close-to-the-ground flowers with blossoms like bells in hues of lavender and violet so intense they make you squint. Pinks and purples and fuchsias and riots of yellows and oranges and crimsons. So much color is making me feel a little well, queasy, and I know I'm on visual overload when I suddenly see the hotel as a gray-painted boat afloat on a ocean of blooms and then a woman in a pale gray dress standing in a field of flowers. I take a couple of steps forward and then the most peculiar thing happens. Maybe it's the effect of the sun or no lunch or my stressful meeting with Barbara, but I actually *swoon*. Really. I get weak in the head, see little black dots in front of my eyes, feel wobbly in the knees, and have to sit down. But where? There, just ahead — the shade of a small planting of pines. I collapse on a bench. Putting my head between my knees, I take deep breaths. And that's how she finds me, gasping for air like a landed trout.

"Are you all right?" a voice asks.

"No, but I'm hoping to be," I say, raising my head cautiously and opening my eyes. I do feel somewhat better, but I'm still not okay, because the woman in front of me seems to be . . . shining. And then I realize that no, of course she's not shining, it's the sun behind her. She steps from the daylight into the shade of the little grove of trees and I see that she does shine, just a little, because she's brought her own brightness with her — short, curly

5

silver hair, to-die-for tanned skin without a single line or a wrinkle, and startling luminous pale gray eyes like cool flames. Her white cotton shirt is rolled up sensibly above her elbows and tucked into a pair of Levi's so faded that they've lost almost every vestige of blue. For a moment, I just gape, because she's . . . perfect. A ten. Absolutely unimprovable.

"Did you walk from the road?" the Shining Woman asks.

"Um, yeah," I answer, still feeling a little vague.

"It's a hot day. C'mon up to the B & B and have a glass of juice."

"Thanks. Maybe in a few minutes," I tell her thinking about the trudge up the hill through the flowers. From someplace close comes the sound of water and I turn, realizing there's a little pond with a small waterfall off to one side. I look more closely and see that in the pond are fish with colors like calico cats. "This place is beautiful," I tell her. "The flowers are, well, amazing, but here, this place, it's . . ." I shrug.

"Someone said it's like being inside a song," she says.

I am surprised. "I know who said that. Samwise Gamgee in *Lord of the Rings*. Only he said it about Lorien, the home of the elves."

"Well, this is Lorien," she tells me.

My grip on reality, never firm at the best of times, slips a little. And then I realize that, of course, Shining Woman is teasing me. "Oh it is, is it?" I tease back. "And here I thought this was Lavner Bay, Oregon."

"No, really, this is Lorien. I'll prove it to you," the woman says and my heart sinks. Here I've met the Woman of my Dreams and she turns out to be, well, a fruitcake. "Come here," she says and holds out her hand.

"Are we going to meet the elves?" I whisper.

She shakes her head, giving me a look that says maybe *I'm* the fruitcake and hope rekindles in my breast. Maybe she isn't wacky. So I take her hand which is warm and fits so very nicely in mine that I admit to myself that crazy or not, I'd follow her anywhere. She leads me over to the pond where the calico fish swim to greet her.

"Look," she says. I look. Into water like black silk. Fish with colors like flames, like January moons, like gold coins rise from the depths. One flips its tail, breaking the surface, and my eyes follow the spreading ring of ripples to the far side of the pond. There, in a bed of moss, is a brass plaque. LORIEN, it says.

"But ... I ..." I turn to her, acutely aware that she is still holding my hand. Who put this plaque here? And what's going on? "This is bizarre ... I mean, this is awfully strange because you see I have a business, well not really a business, actually it's a kind of service that matches up buyers and sellers of rare and out-of-print fantasy and mystery books and, well, I called it Lorien ..." I trail off. Her eyes aren't gray but silver, I decide. "So it's amazing, really amazing that I should find a place, an actual place called Lorien."

"Oh? Is it?" she asks.

"Well, yes. How ... did you put this plaque here?"

She smiles but the smile is a sad smile and I realize that I've asked the wrong question. Broken the mood. She withdraws her hand from mine and now I'm the one who's sad. "Feel better?" she inquires.

Physically I do feel better — certainly less swoony — but psychically, somewhere in the vicinity of my heart, I suddenly feel worse. "Yeah, I feel better," I say because it seems like the thing to do.

"So, c'mon up to the house. You can have that drink. Oh, and we have a room for you."

"A room?"

"Yes. In the B & B. That's what we do — we rent out rooms." Her eyes tease me again and then she's serious, assessing me, I sense. For what, I wonder? Then, like a bolt of lightning on a clear day, it hits me. A horrible *knowledge*.

"The B & B, is it . . . I mean, what's its name?"

"Lavner Bay Bed and Breakfast. Why — are you in the wrong place?"

"Hmm? No, no, of course not," I tell her, fielding my shock like a nimble shortstop. The monstrosity with the gingerbread. Lavner Bay B & B.

My inheritance.

Chapter 2

I sit in a floral print armchair in the lobby of
Lavner Bay B & B, sipping a glass of juice that looks
like wine and tastes like berries, wondering what to
do next. A skinny blonde kid of indeterminate gender,
maybe 10 or 11, sits in an armchair opposite me. It's
dressed in a pair of jeans as ragged as its haircut,
indescribably dirty sneakers, and a once-red T-shirt
bearing Captain Kirk's exhortation: "Beam Me Up,
Scotty."

"Will you be staying?" it inquires politely.

"What? I guess so," I say hesitantly. Why not? I

9

have to stay somewhere and what better place than mine own hostelry. Besides, as I've been sitting here sipping and resting, another idea has occurred to me: maybe I'll just spend a little time here incognito. Check things out. See how well the place is run. Investigate its cash flow. I laugh at this, realizing that I know less about cash and its flow than I do about almost anything else in life. My book business, as much as I love it, will never make me rich. Back in southern California, from whence I hail, I am a card-carrying member of the Working Poor. "If you let me have your car keys we can have your rental brought up to the parking lot," the genderless munchkin offers.

Oh yeah? I look at her/him with southern California suspicion. "And just who are we, pray?" I ask.

"*We* are those of us who work here," he/she says loftily, as though I should have intuited the fact.

I smite myself on the forehead for effect. "Of course," I tell her. "I'm in the habit of handing over my car keys to ten-year-olds. Who's to say you aren't fronting for the local car theft ring? No way, Junior."

The waif slides out of the armchair, gives me a wounded look, and disappears into the bowels of the B & B. I snort. Probably an emissary from the Lavner Bay Chop Shop.

"Ma'am," says a deep voice from behind me, "I'd be happy to drive your car up the hill."

I turn, hoping for the Shining Woman, but she's a tenor, not a bass. The woman who appears from the depths of the B & B is an Amazon, six feet if she's an inch, and admirably endowed with, well, with muscles. She's wearing gray mechanic's overalls, and a yellow tank top which leaves her arms and shoulders bare and I'm carried away with admiration of her biceps. Does she lift weights? I wonder. She must. Tendrils of dark hair escape from her baseball cap and she brushes at them with one wrist. I see why — her hands are absolutely, positively black with gunk.

"Oil," she says, noting my inspection of her hands. "I'm Pan. I work here. I do motors. Right now I'm taking one apart. You can give your car keys to Ossie, my kid. I'll go get your car in a jiffy. Otherwise, you can drive it up the hill yourself." She gives me a very nice, white-toothed smile. "It's up to you."

I feel chastised. "Sure," I say, handing my car keys to the raggedy blonde. It's a girl, I decide. "Sorry," I say to her, then: "Thanks," I tell Pan.

"No problem," she says, giving me an enigmatic look. "C'mon, runt," she says and the kid follows her out, beaming.

I finish my juice and get up to wander around the lobby, hoping my silver-haired hostess will soon return. In the meantime, I admire the oak floor, the overstuffed floral armchairs, the massive table loaded with restaurant menus and guidebooks, and the check-in counter, which consists of a piece of glass atop a huge, many-branched driftwood log. I'm wondering how on earth the log was transported here when I hear footsteps behind me. My heart leaps up, I turn . . . but it's only Ossie.

"Delia asked me to check you in," she says, facing me across the check-in counter. She places a card in front of me with spaces for name, address, license number and so on, and I take the pen she offers me, preparing to write, when caution stays my hand.

"Something wrong?" Ossie inquires.

"Um, no, that is, how much are your rooms?" I ask, to cover up the fact that if I sign in as Allison O'Neil, it won't take anyone very long to figure out who I am and I don't want that. Not just yet.

"The room we have available is eighty-five dollars a night," she tells me.

"Okay," I say, but my mind's such a blank, I can't think of a suitable last name and so I sign a shortened version of my first and middle names: Allie Grace. Maybe that will keep them off the scent for a while. I finish filling out the registration card and hand it back to the kid.

"Allie Grace," she says. "That's a nice name. Grace was the name of the lady who owned this place. She died, though," Ossie says in a small, pinched voice.

"I'm sorry," I say. "What happened."

"She drowned." The kid looks at me solemnly. "I'm not supposed to talk about it though."

"Oh really?" My antennae vibrate.

"Delia says —" She shakes her head firmly. "No," she reiterates, as if to remind herself.

I decide to try a different tack. "Ossie's a nice name," I say. "Is it a family name?"

She gives me an odd, embarrassed look. "It's short for Ocelot. My dad gave us all cat names — my brothers are Tiger, Jaguar, and Cougar. Back in Kansas, we had a garage — you know, we fixed cars. We all worked in it — me and my mom, too."

"Sounds like you miss it."

"Uh huh," she says. "But I work a little here, so it's not so bad."

"So what happened? Did you move?"

She hangs her head. "Not exactly. My mom and I woke up one morning and my dad and brothers were gone."

"Gone? You mean, they just left?"

"Uh huh."

"Where did they go?"

She shrugs. "Mom says they just moved on. So we had to move on, too. She says she doesn't know what happened to them or where they went." She adds in a hushed voice, "But I do."

This is a terrible story and I'm sorry I ever opened up such a can of worms. But I feel trapped now, compelled to carry on. "You do?"

"Yeah. Aliens took them," she says solemnly.

"Aliens," I repeat. "Um, what makes you think that?"

She gives me a cagey look. "I don't know if I should tell you."

"Ossie?" a voice calls and with a start I come back to reality. I realize I was getting into all this *X-Files* stuff and give myself a good mental shake. Jeez, the kid really had me going there for a minute. Aliens, indeed. To my delight, Shining Woman appears behind Ossie and picks up my completed registration card. "Very good," she tells the kid and Ossie smiles shyly. "So, how will you be paying, Allie?" she asks me and, surprised, my heart gives a disconcerting *thump* when I hear her say my name.

"Credit card," I say, rummaging in my backpack.

13

I hand over my Visa card. She runs it through a machine, then gives it back to me along with my car keys.

"Welcome to Lavner Bay," she says. "C'mon. I'll take you upstairs to your room. By the way, my name is Delia."

Delia? She who told Ossie not to talk about Grace's drowning? Hmmm. Very interesting. I follow her obediently as she walks out from behind the registration desk to a staircase beside the front door, trying not to ogle as she walks ahead of me. I'm glad when we come to my room. She unlocks the door and crosses to the far wall to open the curtains and unlatch the window. "This is one of the best rooms," she says, planting one hip on the windowsill and I dutifully look around. Certainly it's large, with a dusty rose-colored Berber carpet, a white chenille bedspread, and wallpaper in some floral design that picks up the rose color in the carpet. The dresser, night table, and bedstead all look as if they're made from cherrywood. I'm pleased — after all, I wouldn't want *my* place to be tacky. But my attention is only half on the furnishings of the B & B. The other half is divided equally between questions that have begun to form in my mind and the unsettling effect that Delia's presence is having on me.

"It has a great view," she offers and I dutifully come forward to appreciate it. She makes no effort to move and I end up standing at the window beside her, appreciating the view of the ocean and inhaling Scent of Delia — something terrific that smells like sandalwood. "So, are you on vacation?" she asks.

I shake my head. "No. Business."

I feel her looking me up and down — my jeans,

14

polo shirt, and Birkenstocks hardly seem like business clothes.

"Family business," I offer.

"Ah," she says. Then: "You know, you look so familiar. Have you ever been here before?"

I start to sweat. Of course I look familiar — I look like Mother, and Mother and Aunt Grace were twins. I wonder how long it will take Delia to figure this out. Not long, I suppose. So I decide to ask my questions now, before my cover is blown. "Nope," I say truthfully. "I've never set foot in Oregon before, let alone in Lavner Bay."

"Oh," she says, but I can see her mental wheels turning nonetheless.

What the hell, I think, and plunge right in with my questions. "Ossie tells me that the former owner drowned. That sounds terrible. Was it long ago?"

She turns from me and looks out the window. "No," she says after a moment. "It was the beginning of last week. About ten days ago."

"Omigosh," I sympathize ingenuously. "What exactly happened?"

"See that rock out there in the bay?"

I look where she's indicating and see a couple of jagged rocks rising maybe twenty feet from the sea. They look like a small mountain range.

"Grace used to take the B & B's Boston Whaler out there and anchor her boat. Then she'd snorkel. Look at the fish and the seals. It was her way of getting some exercise."

"So what went wrong?"

Delia shrugs. "We don't know. She didn't come back for dinner that Sunday, so we started looking for her. When we didn't find her on the grounds, we looked out in the bay. The boat was still anchored there at the rocks. I called the police then. Later . . . the Coast Guard found her on the far side of the rocks."

"Could you tell . . . what happened?"

"Hypothermia. She spent too long in the water. The cold drained her strength. She couldn't get back into the boat. She drowned."

"Are you sure? Was there an autopsy?"

"The medical examiner didn't think there was any need," she says. She turns and looks at me and I realize I've said too much, asked too many questions. But as she turns away, I catch a glimpse of something that looks a whole lot like fear and I realize with a jolt of prescience that this lady's hiding something. Something enormous that makes her feel so guilty she'd love to have the load taken off her shoulders.

"I'm sorry," I tell her with genuine emotion. "Really sorry. You must all miss her. Grace."

Delia doesn't answer for a moment and when she does, she's all business. "Thank you. We do miss her. Well, I'm sure you have things to do — the family business you mentioned."

"Oh, that," I say, barely remembering my lie. "Sure, yeah, I'd better take care of it."

She walks to the door, pauses, then turns around. "It's Friday. We usually barbecue on the back deck. You're welcome to join us if you like. About six o'clock."

"Thanks," I say. "I'd love to."

She closes the door behind her and after she's gone I can still smell her sandalwood soap. Regretfully, I find my nascent fantasies of concupiscence beginning to wither on the vine, replaced, alas, by a meaner growth: budding unease. Not suspicion exactly. Just . . . unease. I wander back to the bed, flop down, run my hands over the pebbly chenille surface, and stare at the ceiling.

Barbecue on the back deck? I'm not a sociable soul, but I wouldn't miss it for the world.

Chapter 3

Lies are the damnedest things, aren't they? Here I am, on the road, driving somewhere, anywhere, to waste time because I fibbed to Delia about the family business that brought me to Oregon. Oh well. So I wheel out of Lavner Bay ("Gem of the Oregon Coast" the Welcome To sign says — ha!) thinking and driving until I realize I can't do both simultaneously without causing an accident. Just inside the town of Windsock, a thriving metropolis of 1,681 people, I see that the view of a pretty bay and a magnificent bridge can be enjoyed from a pocket-sized park right on the sand, so I pull in, greatly relieving the mind of the driver behind me who honks his approval loudly. Oregonians are such testy drivers.

I have to admit it's a darned pretty view. The water in the little bay is a ruffled steely blue today and the sky a powder blue with little puffy white clouds like those cotton balls you buy a zillion to a package for removing makeup. I'm actually zoning out on all this picture-postcard prettiness when the guilty look on Delia's face reenters my mind. Right on the heels of Delia comes the Barbara Bush lookalike and, belatedly, Aunt Grace. I start to feel stressed with all these women rattling around in my head and decide that maybe I ought to have something to eat. After all, it's two in the afternoon and I still haven't eaten anything.

A hut at the corner of a seaside street proclaims itself to be a café, so I walk over there, order a sack of surprisingly good-looking french fries and walk back to my car, eating them. Out on the bay a bunch of little boats work in industrious circles and I figure they must be engaged in crabbing or some other fishy endeavor. I lean against the bumper of my car, nibbling my lunch and, belatedly, admit that trying to pass myself off as someone else at Lavner Bay B & B was a very bad idea. It's only going to take Delia a short time to figure out who Allie Grace is. Especially since my Visa card says Allison Grace O'Neil. I blush, embarrassed by my own stupidity. Hey, I don't write mystery novels, I just sell 'em.

Actually, the Fair Delia knows as much about me as I do about her — she got the same copy of the will as I did. We're both beneficiaries of Aunt Grace's estate: Allison Grace O'Neil gets the B & B and

$10,000, Cordelia Norville gets $10,000, and a bunch of other people get ten grand apiece. It's all there, and I now realize I ought to have perused the damned thing more closely. But I have Document Block — I never have been able to wade my way through forms or official missives. Reluctantly, I retrieve my copy of Aunt Grace's will from my backpack and force myself to study it, curious about the other beneficiaries. Pansy Constantine gets $10,000. Ocelot Constantine gets $10,000 but it's held in trust. My God — Pan and Ossie. Who else gets money? A couple of women named Emily Carsten and Emily Goodrich each get $10,000. I snort at this — Goodrich indeed. Finally, a broad named Gabrielle Fortunata gets $10,000. Then there are a bunch of charities that get a few thousand apiece. I fold the will and put it back in my backpack. It seems that Aunt Grace was a pretty wealthy woman. Well, there's another thing I didn't know about her.

Come to think of it, what do I know about her? Not much.

With a twinge of guilt I realize that I missed my aunt's funeral — actually Barbara Bush said there wasn't a traditional funeral, just a cremation and a memorial service. But I missed it nonetheless. I just couldn't get a flight.

I try to conjure up an image of Aunt Grace and fail. Hell, the last time I saw her was at hers and my mom's 50th birthday party, just before Mom died. That was my last year of college and Mom's illness messed me up so badly that I never did graduate. I recall Aunt Grace writing to me in that horrible year but after a few abortive attempts at replies, all I did was lie on my bed in my college dorm room and read

Lord of the Rings and listen to Bob Dylan's "Sad-Eyed Lady of the Lowlands." I dragged myself out of bed for my Irish poetry class and for the Science Fiction Club's meetings, but pretty soon it became clear even to me that I was wasting my time. Mom had paid my tuition 'til the end of the year so I stayed on, having nowhere else to go. I must have been a pretty spooky sight, hanging out in the college's underground tunnels, hair lank, clutching copies of arcane horror novels gleaned from the local secondhand bookstore. At the end of the year my friends got degrees or husbands or sensible teaching jobs and I got a job in the aforementioned bookstore which enabled me to barely eke out a living. Oh well — at least I didn't have to pay for reading material.

I realize now that Aunt Grace must have been in as much pain as I was — after all, she'd just lost her sister — but selfish turd that I was, all I could think about was myself.

Summoned back to the present by a craving for caffeine and sugar, I walk down the street to a place whose lavender-painted sign says it's The Daily Grind. It has a terrific view of the bay and from the *barista,* a young woman with garnet hair precisely the color of mine, a pale, ethereal complexion, and a black leather jacket, I order a latte and wonder why the hell my aunt left me anything at all. I pay for my drink and am just about to take it out onto the deck when I catch a glimpse of a familiar head of silver hair. I can hardly believe my eyes — it's Delia, sitting at a table with four other women of assorted ages and sizes. Fortunately, she's deep in discussion so she doesn't see me standing in the doorway, gaping like the village idiot. I hastily retreat behind the coffee shop's one indoor plant — an unhealthy but still leafy ficus — and peer through the foliage at the fivesome on the deck.

What, pray tell, is Delia doing here when she was so careful to tell me she had work to do at the B & B? I mean, of course she's entitled to slip out for an afternoon with the girls, but why tell me otherwise? Hmmm. I sip my latte and spy. One of the women, a salt-and-pepper-haired fiftyish woman, puts an arm around Delia and hugs her. Delia puts her head on the woman's shoulder and another of the women, a brunette with glasses, reaches for her hand. Clearly this is a tea and sympathy gathering. But sympathy for what? Now Delia is sobbing, her head in her hands. Embarrassed and confused, I am just about to leave when the blonde and the salt-and-pepper stand, urging Delia to her feet. The others stand also, and I realize the whole bunch is about to leave together; panicked, I look for a place to hide. There, in the corner, a table. I grab one of the local free publications, hurriedly sit down, and hold the paper in front of my face. The group passes within ten feet of me and I hold my breath, expecting detection any instant.

"Eight o'clock, okay?" someone asks.

"I don't know if I can do this," a voice I recognize as Delia's responds.

"You have to. We have to. It's the last thing," the first voice says. I peer around the edge of the paper. It's salt-and-pepper. She puts a hand on Delia's arm. "We're all in this together. Okay?"

"Okay," Delia agrees after a moment. But this is clearly something that doesn't make her happy. "Who's got the, um, Grace's —"

"I do, remember?" the brunette says. "Do you want it?"

"God, no!" Delia says. "I just want to . . . get rid of it. I thought this would be easy, but it's not."

"This has been terrible for you, I know," salt-and-pepper says. "But just hang on a little longer. Okay?"

They murmur agreement to each other, hug, and leave together, the screen door banging shut behind them. I put down the paper, feeling like an actor who's stumbled onto the wrong stage.

What in hell are these women up to? What are they going to do at eight o'clock? And is it eight o'clock today or some other day? Obviously they're going to get rid of something — "the last thing" — but what could that be? And the last thing presumes other, preceding things — things which they were, by their own admission, "in together." Ever one who loves a mystery, I'd be intrigued by all this even if it didn't involve my aunt Grace. My dead aunt Grace, I remind myself.

I fold the paper I'm reading, trying to tell myself that there's undoubtedly some perfectly innocent explanation for what I've heard, but for the life of me, I can't supply one. Assuming tonight's the night (and that's a big assumption), my evening is shaping up to be a busy one indeed.

* * * * *

Showered, blown dry, moussed, clad in a clean black T-shirt and jeans, I'm as presentable as I can make myself. It's five forty-five and I'm pacing the floor in my room at the B & B, trying to talk myself into the proper mood for tonight's events. I study my reflection in the mirror over the dresser, wondering, as I always do, how I'll survive yet another social occasion. I smile, just to remind myself how to do it. I have Mom's bright red hair which I've covered this year with a garnet dye job, never having gotten over being taunted for my carrot top in school. My freckles can't be covered up so I've given up trying. Mom and Aunt Grace had these beautiful green eyes but I've got my dad's muddy brown ones. Mom never talked about Dad — he left us when I was four and I hardly remember him. She changed her name back to O'Neil after he decamped, and when she was forced to refer to him she called him William Martin or Mr. Martin — a strange but effective technique for distancing us psychologically from him. It worked — I've never had a father craving.

I descend the staircase, wondering as I do if Delia lives in the B & B or in town. And presto, as though the thought has conjured her up, here she is at the bottom of the stairs.

"Hi," she says, "I was waiting for you," and my heart does a little hop at the improbability of it. More likely is the fact that she's seen through my little charade and is waiting to accost Allison O'Neil, the Mendacious Heiress. Still, I find myself smiling fatuously.

"You were?" I ask. I'm such a sucker.

"Yes," she says. "I thought I'd introduce you to the others."

Ah yes. Those others. The B & B's guests. I'm a little crestfallen, realizing Delia hadn't been so smitten by my girlish good looks that she'd lingered on the staircase, waiting for me. Instead, I realize she can't wait to pawn me off on the guests. Well, why not? That would free her up for her eight o'clock rendezvous with her friends. "Great," I say, trying to summon up some enthusiasm.

She laughs and I hate it that I've begun to suspect her of something dire. She's the first attractive woman I've met in far too long and dammit, she's ineligible. For one giddy moment I'm tempted to blurt out the Awful Truth, fling myself into her arms, and exchange confessions. I'll fess up to my true identity and she'll tell me that what she and her friends are going to get rid of at eight o'clock is nothing more than a bag of moldy bread for the seagulls. We'll laugh, go to my room, tear each other's clothes off, and engage in a night of amorous athleticism. Right.

"Are there many others coming to the barbecue?" I ask because I have to say something.

"A few. But I might as well tell you — they're not really *guests*," she says.

I'm confused. "They're not really guests? What are they, then?"

"Well, they're residents."

"Residents? As in they live here?"

"Uh huh."

"Oh." Then, because I have to know, I ask, "What about you? Do you live here too?"

She laughs. "Yes. I live here, too."

Well that's good to know. And then my newly acquired business sense kicks in and I'm horrified. "I may be out of line here but wouldn't it be more profitable to rent out the rooms to, you know, guests? Tourists?"

"I suppose so," she says thoughtfully. "But Grace wanted it this way."

What the hell? I can hardly wait to see the B & B's books. And then I realize that I haven't got a clue how to go about this. Where are the books? Who do I ask to see them? And would I know what I was looking at even if I did? A weight begins to settle on my shoulders and I groan.

"Are you all right?" Delia asks.

"Sure. Just a stray thought. That family business I told you about."

"Oh yes. How's it going?"

I bite back a giggle of hysteria. Are we playing doubles? How would I know what she knows about what I know? Especially since her back is turned to me and I can't read her expression. "Let's just say it's going," I answer hoping to put her off by my vagueness.

Fortunately her thoughts are elsewhere because she turns the conversation back to the barbecue. "I'd like you to meet the others," she says. "You're the first real guest we've had in ages." Oh yeah? Why is she so hot to have me meet the others? Why does she care about me? And then it dawns on me — she doesn't. She just needs to keep me occupied.

Out on the deck the sun is blazing. It's nowhere near setting and we'd all fry ourselves alive if it weren't for the nifty awning that Ossie is laboriously cranking over us. Pan goes to help her and soon we're all in the shade which is fortunate because I'm blinking like an owl, having left my sunglasses on my dresser in Lancaster.

There's a little hors d'oeuvres spread set out — some crackers and cheese, an ice bucket with a nice bottle of Chardonnay in it, and an ice chest with Calistoga water and half a dozen Cokes I bet are for Ossie, so I help myself to the Chardonnay and lean against the deck railing, studying the other barbecue attendees. Apart from Pan, Ossie, and Delia, there are a pair of gray-haired elderly ladies with froufrou coiffures and matching floral dresses, and a very tall, skinny, intense-looking young woman with an unfortunate resemblance to Olive Oyl in the Popeye comics. Delia takes me by the elbow and heads me in the direction of the floral dress duo and Olive Oyl.

"Emily Carsten, Emily Goodrich, this is Allie Grace."

The Emilys bob their heads in greeting (I was wrong — they're drinking the Cokes).

"Allie is staying with us — in downstairs east."

"Oooo!" one of the Emilys exclaims. "A guest! How nice!" They then turn back to what was clearly a private conversation, gray heads close together, arms around each other's waists.

I feel rebuffed but Delia tows me down the deck to Olive Oyl, who is busy gnawing a hangnail and crossing and recrossing her legs. She can't be more than twenty-one or so, but the kid is a mess. Her wrinkled khaki shorts belong on a much larger person and her once-white polo shirt is a disgrace. Her hair resembles another comics page regular — Prince Valiant — but hers is a rat's nest of tangles and tufts. Someone really ought to take this babe in hand because I can see that underneath all this static is a potentially gorgeous person. "Gabrielle Fortunata, this is Allie Grace. A guest."

Gabrielle. I realize with a jolt that the gang's all here — Delia, Ossie, Pan, the Emilys, Gabrielle, and me. The beneficiaries of Aunt Grace's estate.

"A guest," says Gabrielle, surprised. "That's, um, nice."

I peer suspiciously at her but she seems absolutely sincere.

Delia wanders off, and Gabrielle twines and gnaws for a few moments until the silence becomes too much for her. "I'm Bree," she blurts out. "Gabrielle's too formal. What do you do? Wherever is it you're from?" she asks.

"Me? Well, I'm from Lancaster — that's in California — and I have my own mail-order book business."

"Oh yeah?" Bree says, peering up at me from under a thicket of bangs. "I have my own business too. That must have been why Delia introduced us."

I'm not sure about that, but I decide to play along anyhow. "What's your business?"

She takes a few good chomps at her thumb and darts me a furtive look. "Cats."

"Cats?"

"Uh huh. I'm a cat writer."

Ye gods, another fruitcake. "A cat writer. That means, what, that you write about cats, you write for cats, you write to cats..." Or for all I know, she writes as a cat. Now *that* would be interesting.

She frowns at my levity. "I write a newsletter on cat behavior. It's called *No Bad Cats*."

"Oh yeah?" I ask. "Maybe I should subscribe. I

have a very bad cat. He prowls all night, sleeps all day, brings home disgusting live things to chase around the house, hoists his leg and cleans his balls on the kitchen counter, and farts under the table when I have dinner guests. Do you think there's any hope for him?"

Bree shakes her head. "I wouldn't call him bad. He seems . . . pretty normal to me. You might get him a few toys, though. He sounds bored."

I laugh, Bree laughs, and suddenly I realize that she's not a fruitcake at all. She's just shy. And a little weird. And for all I know she hates these social situations more than I do. "Say, can I get you a glass of Chardonnay?" I ask her.

She's clearly stunned. "I, that is, sure."

Delia's deep in conversation with Pan and as I pass them on my way to the ice bucket, they fall silent. Interesting. I wonder if Pan is in on the Eight O'clock Caper. I bring Bree her glass of wine and we sit in the shade.

"So what brought you to Lavner Bay?" I ask her.

"Vet school," she blurts out. "I'm a vivisection dropout. I ran as far as I could from college. In Florida. When I stopped running, I found myself here. The top lefthand corner of the map."

Surprise — I'm beginning to like Bree. "And then what?"

She shrugs. "I rented a room here, ran out of money, had a nervous breakdown, got my head on straight again thanks to Grace, and stayed."

Ah, Grace again. I decide to play dumb. "Grace. Wasn't she the manager of this place?"

She shakes her head. "No. The owner."

"People sure seem to have liked her."

Bree's eyes fill with tears. "They loved her," she whispers, her voice choked, and I feel like a worm. But I have to press on.

"What exactly happened to her? I heard she drowned."

Bree's eyes register guilty alarm and she hastily plunks her wineglass down on the table between us. She blinks several times, crosses her arms, gnaws her thumb, and winds her legs around each other. Boy, talk about nervous. "Yeah, she drowned," Bree says evasively. "But I really don't know any more about it." Her gnawing has drawn blood and she notices, hastily wiping her thumb on her shorts.

I take pity on her and change the subject. "So did everyone come here the way you did — Pan, Ossie, the two flower ladies? And what about Delia?"

Bree smiles. "The flower ladies. I like that. We call them the Emilys. Yeah, I guess they all just . . . drifted here. Like me. The Emilys came as tourists. Let's see if I can get this straight. They'd always been best friends. One of them was married to the other one's brother and when he died, they went back to being inseparable. Pan came here when her husband left her and Ossie — her car literally blew up on the lane leading to the B & B. Scared Grace and Delia half to death. And me you know about."

"What about Delia?" I prodded.

She frowns. "I'm not sure. She was Grace's manager. They were pretty close. That's about all I know."

I raise an eyebrow. "Close?"

Bree blushes. "Well, they seemed to be good friends. I don't think there was anything more between them. Although this is certainly the place for it."

I'm lost. "The place for it?"

Bree smiles a cat's smile, full of secrets. "Didn't you notice all the lavender mailboxes and doors as you drove into town? Out of town, for that matter too."

"Well, yeah," I admit. "So what?"

She looks at me in amusement. "You really don't get it, do you?"

I'm beginning to feel a little irritated. "Nope. I really don't get it."

"I'll give you a clue. Lavner Bay's nickname is Lavender Bay."

Lavender Bay. Is she kidding? "Lavender? You mean —" I stop, not wanting to step in it.

Bree nods, delighted. "Half the women in town are, well, lavender," she declares in self-satisfaction, and with that assertion, I have to sit down. The prospect is stunning. "Half the women? You mean there are, well, a hundred and fifty . . ." I fumble for the most politically correct word to use.

"Sisters," Bree supplies.

"Sisters, yeah. So there are, like, a hundred and fifty sisters here?"

"Welllll," Bree amends. "In town and up and down the coast a few miles. And inland a little."

"Yikes," I say.

And then I wonder: why is she telling *me* this? Is she a sister? Does she think I'm one? I gulp my wine, suspecting that the answer to both of these questions is yes and not knowing what to say about either to a near stranger. So I change the subject back to what really interests me — Aunt Grace's death. Maybe I can get this ditzy babe to talk now that she thinks (I guess) that we're sisters.

"Well, that's pretty interesting," I say, acknowledging her revelation about the lavender sisters of Lavner Bay, "but I'm a little confused."

"Oh, you are?" she asks earnestly, thinking no doubt that I'm about to bare my soul. Ha. Fat chance.

"Yeah. If Delia was Grace's companion — you know, her friend — why on earth would she have let her go swimming in the ocean alone? I mean it's cold, isn't it? And that rock is pretty far out there. And Grace wasn't exactly young."

Bree crosses her arms and hunches over as if she's hugging a secret to her breast. Which, I realize, she is. Dammit, this kid knows something. Just like Ossie knows something and Delia knows something. Something they don't want to talk about.

"Bree?" I ask but she says nothing, rocking silently in reply. Suddenly I'm tired of this. I get up, pour myself another glass of Chardonnay, and walk down the steps to the path that leads to edge of the cliff. To hell with these crazy women.

There's a bench just off the path, with a terrific view of the little cove, and I carry my wine over there, intending to sit down. As I do, I notice a brass plaque affixed to the bench and bend to read it. *This bench is provided so everyone can enjoy this view as much as Caroline did.* Oh God. I sit cross-legged on the grass. Not another dead woman. What happened to *her*? Did she fall off the cliff? Uneasy, I stand up and peer over to the little pebble beach about twenty feet below me. The distance hardly looks lethal. A fall from this height would only give you a wrenched ankle. At the most a broken one. I sit back down on the grass feeling suddenly tired. Tired from traveling, tired from trying to digest today's array of information, and tired of these women. My head feels as though it's full of bees. Draining my wineglass, I stretch out in front of Caroline's bench and close my eyes. Rest. I need rest. Then I'll go back to the barbecue and tackle these females again, but first, rest. I close my eyes.

"Allie? Allie? Are you okay?" Someone is pawing at my shoulder and I brush the paw away. Must be Sam Spade, plucking at my pj's to urge me to get up. But Sam doesn't usually call my name, at least not in English, so, curious, I open my eyes. A woman resembling Olive Oyl is bending over me and my brain places me on the grass at Lavner Bay, not in my comfy bed in Lancaster.

"Shit," I say grumpily, aggrieved that if someone had to come and shake me awake, why couldn't it have been Delia? Of course, I might have flung myself upon her in a fit of unfettered lust, so it's probably just as well that Bree is doing the shaking.

"I was worried," Bree says apologetically. "I noticed that you had three glasses of wine and well, the cliff edge is a little unstable here, and —"

"Enough," I tell her. "Thanks for caring, though."

"Look," Bree says in a hushed voice. "The sun is just about to set."

I sit up, run my hands over my face and through my hair (yes, I do feel as though I've had three glasses of wine), and look out to sea. Sure enough, there's the sun, as big and shiny as a brass gong, about to disappear behind the rim of the world.

"I never get tired of looking at it," she says and out of deference to her sense of aesthetics, I keep quiet. As we look, the sun drops out of sight, leaving a pink pervasive glow that makes Bree sigh. "Beautiful," she says and I have nothing to say in return. I feel that I've failed Sunset Appreciation 100. Sure it's pretty, but, I mean, how exciting can a sunset be? "Allie," she says at last, having exhausted the sunset's potential, "I want to tell you something." I perk up at this.

"Yeah?" I say encouragingly.

"Grace O'Neil's death, well, it affected us all deeply. And it was so . . . recent. I can't talk to you about it now. Do you understand?"

What can I say? "Oh sure," I tell her reassuringly. "It was no big deal. I was just curious. Besides who am I — just a B & B guest, right?"

We laugh at this, and after we're done, Bree shakes her head. "Something tells me that you're not just a guest," she says and my stomach clenches in alarm.

"Oh yeah? What am I then?"

"I can't say," she says, pulling up little tufts of grass and letting them blow away in the breeze that has sprung up. "But all of us came here for a reason. Why not you?"

"I came here for a reason all right — a room," I scoff, trying to get her off this track.

"No, I'm serious. Lots of people come here for rooms, but I sense something . . . different about you."

I blush to the roots of my garnet curls and thank heaven for the concealing twilight. "Nah," I tell her. "It's your imagination."

"Nope," she says definitely. "I'm never wrong about these things."

"Well, time will tell, I suppose," I say platitudinously. "C'mon, let's see about that barbecue."

It's a salmon, a whole one, for God's sake, and it's huge. At least two feet long. Do they really grow that big? I'm terribly impressed. Ossie is very carefully carrying the platter on which the aforementioned fish reposes and she smiles in triumph as she deposits it safely on the table. Gone are the Cokes, wine, and hors d'oeuvres, to be replaced by something that looks like potato salad, a big bowl of marinated veggies, and two loaves of bread. A feast, my stomach proclaims, gurgling in anticipation.

"Please," Delia says, motioning me to a chair, and I realize this is to be a sit-down dinner. Places have been set around the table and lanterns lighted on the deck railings. We take our places — Pan, Ossie, and Bree on one side of the table, me at one end, and the Emilys on the other side. Once the shuffling of bodies and chairs is over, I realize with a start that there's no place for Delia.

"I'm not going to join you," Delia says, putting a hand on Ossie's head. "I'm feeling rather . . . tired."

Ever solicitous, Bree murmurs and looks up at her.

"Go to bed," one of the Emilys says. "We'll be thinking of you, dear," the other replies.

"I think I will go to bed. Enjoy yourselves. Tell our guest some stories about the coast. Maybe she'll want to stay." She kisses Ossie's cheek and then, before I can say a thing, she's gone. I check my watch. Twenty to eight. Frustrated, I help myself to potato salad and mentally congratulate Delia for orchestrating this little soirée so nicely. What can I do — faint? Plead a similar case of fatigue? Hardly. I help myself to potato salad and fulminate.

Now it's midnight and Delia still isn't back. I know this because I'm lurking on the front steps of the B & B where I can't possibly miss her car. Where in hell did she go? What's taking her so long? And what was she up to with the ladies I saw at the coffeehouse? I yawn, pulling my sweatshirt sleeves down over my hands. It may be summer, but the night is pretty darned chilly. I'm so tired I can hardly keep my eyes open, so when a car turns onto the B & B's little lane, I jump a foot, realizing that I've been dozing. Sure enough, it's the little white Honda I saw Delia get into at the coffeehouse. The moon is up now and by its light I recognize Delia's profile as the car rounds the corner of the B & B, heading for the parking area in back. Great. Now what? Do I run inside and pretend to be coming down the stairs just as she's going up? Plead insomnia? I snort. Plead insanity is more like it. For a few more minutes I just sit on the porch, listen to the crickets, and watch the moon climb higher in the sky. And fume a little more. Then, because I can't think of anything else to do, I get up, stretch, and go inside to bed.

I'm at the beach, playing in the sand with a pail and shovel, the ocean at my back, little tongues of water sneaking between my feet now and then. The day is hot.

"Stay away from the water, Allison," my red-headed mother calls from the shade of a beach umbrella not too far away.

"The tide's coming in. Come back a little, dear," says Aunt Grace, my mother's double.

Ever the dutiful child, I pick up my pail and shovel and toddle back up the sloping beach toward them. Mother smiles, shading her eyes, reaching out a hand for me. I stop, hunkering down to look at a pretty shell, and then I hear her scream. Surprised, alarmed, I look up and she's standing, frozen in one spot, her hand on her heart, staring at something over my shoulder. I turn to look and see something I don't understand — a wall of water, a wave as tall as a tree, a wave with a top like white horses' manes. I laugh in a mixture of fear and delight as the blue-green wall of water rears up over me then falls with a crash and suddenly I'm being tumbled over and over like clothes in a dryer, water in my eyes and nose, my knees and elbows scraped raw on the pebble beach, and now I really am terrified and as I open my mouth to scream, to call for my mother, water rushes in and I choke, screaming and coughing, until finally I don't cough anymore.

Suddenly something, someone, grabs my hair and I'm yanked out of this cold, quiet green place into sunlight and air and noise. This rough someone is joined by others who turn me facedown to the water and smack me on the back, then turn me over so I'm blinded by the sun. I want to cry out, to tell them to stop, but there's something in my mouth, in my throat.

"Her lungs are full of water," a voice says. "Call for help. I'll work on her," and I feel myself dropped to the sand and turned roughly over.

"C'mon baby, c'mon Allie, cough, breathe, dammit," my aunt Grace says and I want to, but I can't. She keeps pushing on my back and suddenly from somewhere deep inside it's like a bubble bursts and a wave of water rushes out of my mouth. I gag and cough, and then start to breathe in whoops and this scares me so much I start to cry.

"Thank God, thank God," my mother cries and at that, I cry harder, whooping and wailing.

"For God's sake, shut up, Maureen," Aunt Grace says. "You're terrifying her." Then to me: "Allie, you're okay, but you have to stop crying. Just breathe, all right?"

Without my mother screaming and carrying on, I calm down and pretty soon Aunt Grace stops pushing on my back. She helps me to sit up and when I do, I feel so dizzy I throw up.

"Oh God, oh God," my mother starts again.

"It's okay," my aunt tells me, wiping my face with a towel and wrapping me in another one. From someplace we hear the wail of a siren.

"Now we're going for a ride in an ambulance. We're going to the hospital, just to see what that nasty old wave did to my favorite niece," says Aunt Grace. "Allison, do you want Mom to carry you?"

I shake my head. Is she kidding? My aunt is my savior, my champion. Not only did she pluck me from the water but she brought me back to life. What did my mother do except scream and cry? I cling harder to Grace. "No!" I say forcefully.

All three of us climb into the ambulance and when we're settled and on our way, siren screaming, my mom asks Aunt Grace a question.

"That was very brave, Grace. I didn't know you could swim like that."

Aunt Grace laughs. "Swim? Me? I just waded in. Luckily she was right underneath me. I grabbed for her and got her hair. Then I pulled like hell." I can feel her start to shiver. "And it wasn't brave. I'm scared to death of the water. I can't swim a stroke. Never could. Always wanted to learn, though." Her teeth start to chatter, she hugs me hard, I hug her back, and we both burst into tears at the same moment.

"It's okay, kiddo," she says. "You can cry now."

* * * * *

I surface from my dream with a yell, realize where I am, and clamp my hands over my mouth. I'm not buried under tons of water, I'm not even in

39

the ambulance with Aunt Grace and my mother — I'm in bed in Lavner Bay, Oregon, in the business which my aunt left me. After she drowned. I sit up and hug my knees, a horrible realization coming over me. Unless things had changed drastically for Grace — some heavy-duty therapy for her fear of water and some swimming lessons — the likelihood of her having drowned while snorkeling was nil. Oh she drowned all right — I believed that — but what was she doing in the water? Water which, the last time I knew about it, she feared? I pull the blankets up around my chin, realizing that I'm way, way out of my depth. And then, because the image is so bizarre, I start to laugh, but the laughter quickly turns to tears. Help, I call silently, drawing the blankets protectively up to my chin. I need help.

Chapter 4

My night of revelation over, I've fled the B & B for the anonymity of a coffee shop in Windsock. I'm now about 10 miles down the highway from Lavner Bay, in sight of a bridge over what are clearly troubled waters. The sight suits me just fine as I'm more than a little troubled myself. Yesterday's picture-postcard blue sky is gone, replaced by a palette of grays — opal sky, dove gray clouds, pewter water, and a feisty little wind that is whipping up whitecaps in the bay.

"Looks like rain," I offer as the waitress comes to refill my coffee cup.

"Uh huh," she says cheerfully. "But that's why Oregon is so green, isn't it?"

The botany lesson concluded, she's off to dispense coffee and cheer to other customers. I cut my waffles thoughtfully and review my options. One, go home and ignore everything. Two, go home and let a local realtor list the B & B. (This option, I admit, has a whole lot of appeal.) Three, stay and try to figure things out myself. Four, stay and hire someone to try to figure things out. I suppose there might be five, six, and seven, but the quartet of options I've identified seem adequate. I sigh, realizing that after last night's dream, I'm already committed to opening Door Number Four.

There's a phone book lying on the counter by the cashier and I borrow it, signaling the waitress for more coffee. With sinking heart, I see that the book is a distressingly slim volume, but I open it hopefully to Investigators. Alas, there are only four. The ad that immediately catches my eye is a fancy, two-color announcement for the services of C R & M Investigations. They specialize in civil/criminal, photography/video, surveillance, executive protection and process serving. "Serving Oregon since 1956," the ad proclaims. Wow. I'm impressed. And intimidated. Somehow C R & M doesn't seem quite the firm for me. Probably expensive. And they're in Landlubber City, wherever that is. Then there's Tracker Investigations (are they kidding?) and an outfit called The Wheelers Investigative Services (as in wheelers and dealers?). I'm getting a little giddy by this point so when I notice an entry I've overlooked, Coast Investigations, I feel reassured. At least it's not suggestive. Or intimidating. And it's local — the telephone prefix is the same as the B & B. I fortify myself with a little more caffeine and take a quarter over to the pay phone. Expecting to get a recorder, I'm surprised when the phone is answered by a real person. At least I think it's a person.

"Coast," a gravelly baritone growls.

"Ah, er, I'd like to speak to someone about um, an investigation," I stammer.

"Huh. Okay. Just a minute," the voice says and I hear the rustle of a hand covering the receiver. After a moment, another voice comes on the line, similar to the first, but tenor. Either Mr. Coast has cleared a massive hairball from his throat or this is Coast Junior. "This is Kerry," the voice says. "What can I do for you?"

I'm encouraged. A dad-and-son affair could be good. Dad's experience and son's energy. Besides, Kerry is a nice name. "I need some help with a problem. I wonder, could I come in and talk to you?"

Silence. Then: "Let me look at my calendar. When did you want to come in?"

"Well, I know it's a bit of a rush, but today. Soon, if possible."

"Well, the thing is we're kind of . . . committed for the next few days."

"Oh," I say, disappointment evident in my voice. I'm already trying to decide between the Trackers and the Wheelers.

A sigh from Kerry. "Listen. I can give you maybe half an hour if you can get here right away. Otherwise, it'll be the end of the week."

"I can leave right now," I babble gratefully. "Where exactly are you?"

"On the bayfront. Right beside the crab ring rental place. Little blue house."

I'm excited. Kerry is maybe five minutes from where I'm standing. Never mind that I haven't the foggiest what a crab ring is or why one would want to rent one. I mean, do you rent onion rings? Still, I feel it best to project optimism. "I can find it. I'm on my way," I tell him.

Crab rings are not edible. I discover this fact as I park at the public dock, right across from the ramshackle wooden hut that rents them. Crab rings are, rather, round wire contraptions made for hurling or dropping into the water and luring crabs into their escape-proof interiors. The rental hut is doing a brisk business — lots of shorts-and-T-shirts tourist types laden down with the aforementioned rings are lugging them to the end of the wooden pier and tossing them off. I look around for the little blue house. Nothing. There's a cute little slate blue bungalow to the north of the crab ring rental but that can hardly be it — it's a restaurant. Coast Seafood House, the sign says: "Fish so fresh the ocean hasn't missed it yet." Yuk, yuk. If this is the investigator's place, it's another case of Oregonians being color-blind. First the B & B and now this. What is it with these people — has all the rain shorted out their optic nerves? I see movement in the Seafood House so I climb the steps and go on in.

"We're not open yet," says a sharp-eyed Native American woman, her long iron-gray hair twisted into a braid behind her head. She comes to the door not to greet me, I see, but to bar my way. Stout, short, and gnarled, she's clearly a senior, but she's just as clearly the boss here. "We open at eleven," she tells me, standing in my path like a tree stump. "You come back at eleven." I'm beginning to get a little irked. Boss or not, she could use a lesson in PR.

"Sorry," I tell her. "I was looking for Coast Investigations."

She sticks her chin out like an aging pugilist. "Coast Investigations?"

"Yeah. I'm supposed to meet someone named Kerry."

Belligerence turns to disapproval and she skewers me with an evil look. "Upstairs." She points to a staircase in the corner of the restaurant. "There."

"Thanks," I tell her, heading for the stairs, not sure how I've offended her.

"Investigations, ha!" she mutters under her breath and I wonder what I'm getting into. Still, I'm here, Kerry is evidently here, so I decide what the heck. I can always leave and throw myself on the mercy of the Trackers.

Upstairs I find three closed doors opening off a central hall. A window at the end gives enough light for me to see that one door isn't really closed, it's ajar, and so I knock on it tentatively.

"Come," a voice says in an emulation of that affected summons offered by Captain Jean Luc Picard on *Star Trek: The Next Generation*. I stifle a giggle. Inside is a desk whose top is absolutely bare, a straight-backed chair in front of the desk, and a glowering young woman in a uniform standing against the wall. I notice she's leaning heavily on a cane. "You are?" she asks in a continuation of her Jean-Luc persona.

"Allison O'Neil," I say, determined not to show how unnerved I am by all this nonsense. "And you are?"

"Owyhee."

"Excuse me? Hawaii?"

She snorts laughter. "Oh-wy-hee. It's a Native American name. Sit down."

I look around. "Where?"

She grimaces, props her cane against the wall, and moves the room's single chair around to the front of the desk for me. "There," she says, motioning me into it. Reluctantly, I sit. She resumes her post by the window and regards me balefully. I decide to get on with it. "I'm supposed to meet a man named Kerry here."

"Hmmph," she says, raising an eyebrow. She is, I note, a decided improvement on the woman downstairs. Hair as black as a starling's wing, eyes like gourmet Belgian chocolate, gorgeous tan complexion, teeth that could do television commercials. She's gorgeous. Or could be if she weren't scowling so fiercely. "I'm Kerry," she says. "Kerry Owyhee."

"I see," I answer feebly. "Coast Investigations, right?"

She nods, consulting her watch. "You have fifteen minutes. Remember? I said I had —"

"A full calendar. Yeah, I remember." I get to my

feet. As a matter of fact I had completely forgotten, but I'm glad she's giving me an out. Because that's where I want. "Look, I was just thinking that maybe I should go somewhere else. I mean —"

"My office seems awfully *clean* for someone in this line of work, why am I dressed in this funny uniform, who is that witch downstairs, and how could I possibly be an investigator because I'm *disabled*?" She delivers the last word in a stage whisper and I'm not sure if I'm supposed to laugh or run. "Is that what you were just thinking?

"Um, no, not at all," I lie, wondering if I could just make a rush for the door.

"Yes you were," she says, seeing through my lie. "To answer the questions you didn't ask — my office is so clean because I've just moved here; I'm wearing this funny uniform because my aunt got me a job as a security guard at the casino; the old lady downstairs is the aforementioned aunt who heartily disapproves of me; and yes, I am disabled although I hope it's temporary and it has nothing at all to do with my professional competence. I have a P.I. license and a degree in criminal justice, although the latter seems to be a handicap if you'll pardon the pun. Not that I don't have others, mind you." She glares at me again, daring me to contradict her. Not a chance. I'm on information overload and couldn't rise to the bait if I wanted to.

"So how much does Coast Investigations charge?" I ask blandly.

She blinks. Clearly she expected another response. "Oh. Well, the going rate is two-fifty a day. I'd need a two-day retainer to start. If I decide to take your case." She points to the cane. "I'm . . . not very mobile these days, so if it's pavement-pounding you want, you'll have to go somewhere else."

Do I need pavement-pounding? I haven't the faintest idea. So I pretend to do a little mental calculation. After all, Ms. Coast doesn't know I'm an heiress. "I guess I could give you five hundred."

She blinks again, deflated, and when she answers, most of the challenge has gone out of her voice. She's younger than I first thought — about my age, I guess. Which doesn't excuse her acting like a storm trooper, but I figure I might have a better rapport with her than with the Trackers. I mean, like the ad says, they've been serving Oregon since before I was *born,* for cripe's sakes. And she clearly feels defensive about her disability. So I decide to cut her some slack. After all, it's her brain I'll be hiring, right?

"What would I be investigating?" she wants to know.

Ah yes. That. "I can't tell you about it in fifteen minutes. It's . . . complicated."

Kerry looks duly chastened. "I meant what I said about only having a few minutes to talk to you. I have to go to work." Then a thought occurs to her. "But I get lunch at one. We could talk then. If you're still interested."

I consider this. Am I still interested? A testy, disabled, female Native American investigator with several chips on her shoulder — not exactly what I had in mind. Oh, what the heck. She *does* have a P.I. license, so she presumably knows what she's doing. "I'm still interested. Tell me where."

"The gaming center just north of Landlubber City. Salmon Breezes. I'll meet you at the front door."

"Okay," I say, turning to go.

"Hey," she calls as I'm almost out the door, and I turn back, assuming it's me she's addressing. I'm getting used to her abrasive manner, I realize. "My life has been turned upside down. It's making me crazy." I think this is Kerry Owyhee's version of an apology, and I wonder how I'm supposed to respond. I decide to ignore it.

"See you at one," I say and close the door behind me. As I pass through the restaurant, a quartet of Kerry's relatives — two males and two females — give me a matched set of frowns. Presumably they think I'm a bad influence on Kerry, leading her astray or somewhere worse, offering her money to do all those unethical things that Hollywood P.I.s do, making her jaded. I have to laugh at that, because what in hell do they think a job in a casino will do for her outlook on life? Eight hours a day every day watching people stuff dollar after dollar into machines when most of the world is hungry is bound to make one a little warped. Besides, there's all that smoke to contend with, too. If ennui doesn't get you, lung cancer will. Nope, Kerry will be much better off making her living as a P.I. I mean, look at the Trackers. They've been around forever.

"Thanks," I tell them breezily. "Have a nice day."

I have a few hours to kill, so I decide to wander up the coast, playing tourist. The town of Nautilus, which I come upon after only 20 minutes of driving, strikes me as not particularly prepossessing until I realize that it's a real town filled with real businesses where people work and buy stuff — not a tourist trap.

Signs direct me to Nautilus' Historic Bayfront which is, I suppose, Tourist Mecca, but a detour seems a lot of trouble, so I pass, grabbing a café mocha at a drive-through espresso hut and carrying on out of town, through Gemstone Beach and Sea Lion Rock, for parts unknown. The scenery is spectacular — oceans of ocean, sandy beaches the color of *café au lait* on my left, forest in a hundred shades of green on my right. For once, I seem to be driving the right speed so no one's honking at me and I hum Seal's "Kiss From a Rose" as I drive up over Cape Grim (is this a joke?), past a couple of absolutely stunning bays named Crab Claw Cove and Little Crab Claw Cove, and into Drizzle Bay, which calls itself "The Whale Watching Capital of the World." This is not a town but a townlet, and one so small that if you sneezed driving through, you'd miss it, but it seems to be a burg with an attitude. I mean, imagine having the nerve to call yourself the capital of anything when your main street is two blocks long. Feeling a kinship with such bravado, I decide to park and take a look around.

Most of the town's shops are on the east side of the highway — no doubt so tourists can get a good look at those whales off the bridge and breakwater — so I park in front of the caramel corn place, put on a pair of sunglasses I bought at the coffee shop this morning, and mosey down the street. Not surprisingly, it's the typical assortment of tourist shops — T-shirts, souvenirs, postcards — plus a pretty nice gift and art gallery and a few restaurants, but I pass them up, grabbing an ice cream cone and darting across the street to look down at what proclaims itself to be "the world's smallest harbor." It is alarmingly small, I think, gawking over the stone railing with folks from Idaho and Wisconsin, amazed that anyone would try to navigate a boat through a channel that seems no bigger than my living room. But even as I think it, here comes a boat under the bridge, bobbing on the swells, heading out to sea with a load of fisherfolk or whale-watchers. I watch them for a while, but all that pitching and heaving makes me queasy and I toss the remains of my fudge ripple cone into the trash, intending to go back to my car and continue on down the highway. Then a kid yells "Whales!" in a delighted soprano and everyone looks where he's pointing, out to sea, of course, but over to the right, which is, I guess, north. At first I can't see anything, but I squint my eyes and suddenly a slick black ... thing surfaces, as huge and stealthy as a submarine, and sighs a great geyser of air and water. I mean, it's so close we can all hear the *whoosh*. Kids "Oh!" in delight as the thing glides along — sleek, black, mysterious, a citizen of another world — and then it dives, flipping its tail fins at us exactly as if it knew we were there watching it. "Wow!" I say, laughing along with everyone else.

We scan the ocean for a while, but there's nothing happening, so in ones and twos, people drift off to other entertainment. I stay put, though, staring out to sea. Seeing the whale has made a big impression on me and I want a chance to savor the experience, to turn it over in my mind. Remembering the immense back of the whale, I feel a little shiver of awe. I mean, we hunted them almost to extinction — a life form that was old when we were still hauling ourselves out of the primal ooze — but they're still here, and now that we've mostly stopped butchering them, they seem to be actively curious about us. There's a lesson in this, but for which one of us?

I look out to sea, still thinking of whales, and remember an otherworldly bit of information gleaned from the *News Times*. Apparently Keiko the whale, star of the movies *Free Willy* and *Free Willy II*, is being delivered by UPS cargo plane to his new home in Nautilus. That ought to be quite a delivery. The poor guy was captured when he was two and has lived his life at a Mexico City Sea World in a pool he can hardly turn around in. Old and ill, he's coming to Oregon for some much needed R & R, having been purchased by a foundation which fund-raised and built him a magnificent pool five times the size of his present digs, complete with water jets, temperature controls, and two permanent caretakers. It's amazing what guilt will make us do, isn't it? As if all this could atone for the sin of having captured him in the first place.

Chapter 5

I pull into the parking lot for Salmon Breezes
about quarter to one, find a parking space about half
a mile away, and walk to what I take is the front
door. I understand that the casino is only in
temporary quarters here, pending Landlubber City's
approval of a more permanent location, and I have to
admit that its temporary quarters is rather peculiar — an enormous white tentlike structure, smack in
the middle of a parking lot, nestled up to a high-rise
hotel. The structure bears an unnerving resemblance
to a gigantic pale mushroom — something I've heard

Oregon is famous for. However, the city fathers and mothers are apparently less concerned about the aesthetics of the casino than about the usual array of associated ills — increased traffic, increased crime, increased gambling addictions — but I think the town's gotten exactly what it deserves. I mean, after all these years, when we whites thought we had the Indians under control, here they are, the pesky red devils, scalping us again. Seems like poetic justice to me.

Contrary to my expectations, the day has turned out to be beautiful (another of the 82) so why, I wonder as I poke my nose inside the casino's doors, why is this place full of people? I mean, it's packed. I look around, amazed. What a joke — all these vacationers longing for the beach and they choose to spend a day (or more, for all I know) of their holiday in this dark, cavernous space, elbow to elbow with people they would normally cross the street to avoid, their ears besieged with cacophony — I mean if people had to *work* in conditions like this, they'd have a union faster than you can say jackpot. And then I realize that people do have to work here. People like Kerry.

And here she is, squeezing her way through folks piled two-deep at the slot machines, her usual glower in place. She stops, looks around, and seeing me, tries to hurry. But her cane and the press of people make for slow going, which only makes her glower more. *Chill out,* I want to tell her.

"Hi," she says, a note of pleased surprise in her voice and I realize she really did think I wouldn't show.

"Thought I'd stand you up?" I ask as we fight our way out of the casino into the parking lot.

She makes a face. "I wouldn't blame you. I came on a little strong this morning."

"Well, maybe a little," I agree.

She holds up a bag. "I bought a couple of drinks and some sandwiches. To make amends. I thought we'd walk down to the beach and sit on a log while we talk business."

"That sounds nice," I say and she leads the way through the parked cars to a high-rise hotel right on the water. We take a little path around the side of the hotel and there's the ocean, so blue and sparkly that it almost makes you want to live here. Almost. At the far end of the beach are some driftwood logs and we make our way toward them. Kerry sits on a log as big around as a Sumo wrestler, handing me our lunch bag, taking off her jacket and folding it neatly beside her. She's wearing a long-sleeved white shirt and a black tie and, I note with interest, a gun. She unbuckles the gunbelt, sighs, and puts the gun on top of the jacket. Then she rolls up her sleeves and loosens her tie, leaning back, letting the sun shine on her face. It's a gorgeous face, I note again, reminiscent of Joan Baez in her younger days. Feeling like a voyeur, I look away. "Help yourself to lunch," she says. "I have to unwind a little first."

"You don't like the casino job very much, do you?" I ask, rummaging in the bag. I pull out a Diet Coke and a turkey sandwich.

"I don't like it at all. Unlike most of my people, I'm ambivalent about this whole business of Indian casinos." She glowers at the ocean as if to communicate her displeasure. "And it's hell when everyone knows the only reason you've been hired is because your family got the job for you."

"So what would you be doing instead — investigating?"

"Yeah. I've always been the black sheep of the family. Marching to the beat of a different drummer." She looks at me sidelong. "That's an Indian joke. I'm allowed to make them."

"Oh," I say, off-balance.

"Yeah, I'd be investigating," she repeats. "Like I said, I have a license, and I have a couple of years working for Pinkerton's under my belt." She throws a bread crust to some hopeful gulls and is quiet for so long that I wonder what's wrong. Was I supposed to say something? "Dammit, I thought I could . . . bluff my way through this, but I can't," she says. "I'd better tell you the whole thing. I do have a P.I. license — it's based on my hours of work for Pinkerton's. But that work was mostly research — you know, digging through records and so on." She gives a strange little laugh here. "I loved it. I love digging — sifting through documents, looking for connections. I'm not good with people — you know, trying to get them to talk. Unless it's over the phone." She looks off at the ocean. "Anyway, the folks at Pinkerton's were smart enough to put me where I could be most successful. In the back room with three phone lines, a fax, and a computer. It was great. I loved it. I was terrific at my job — got them what they wanted. And then my house was burned down."

I'm horrified. "What?"

"Yeah. It was during my last job for Pinkerton's.

56

A bunch of us were doing research for them — trying to find out if work done on the big new convention center had been done by unlicensed labor. My job was to look at the electrical contracts." She laughed again. "Do you know the damned fire alarms weren't even hooked up?"

I whistled. "Wow."

"Yeah, right," she said ruefully. "It took literally months of sifting through work orders and invoices and so on, and some pretty interesting phone calling, but I found it."

"It?"

"What we needed to find — the smoking gun. I found that the guys who had installed the fire alarm system were day laborers that the electrical contractor had hired off the street. The state hit the electrical contractor with a humongous fine. Put him out of business. Ruined him. So I guess he turned around and hired someone to find out who had fingered him and to administer appropriate punishment."

"Seems a little extreme — burning your house down."

She laughs. "I don't think that's all the little weasel who did it had in mind. I was trapped in the house — I almost died in the fire. So here I am. Working in a casino at the beach."

"Pinkerton's didn't can you, did they?" I asked, horrified.

"What? Oh. No. But after my house burned down and my car was trashed, I got the message — get out of Dodge." She shrugged.

"Insurance?" I asked.

"Yes, thank God. I filed a claim. The adjuster

57

adjusted. That was quite a few months ago. Supposedly the check will be here any day." She threw some more bread to the gulls. "My cousin Daniel won't like it — he's playing the role of protective male — but I plan to rent a place of my own with the insurance money. Open my own agency. My aunt will be delighted, however."

"Your aunt —the one you called the witch?"

Kerry grimaced. "Yeah. When I came to the coast and needed a place to stay, well, she didn't want to help me. It's a long story. Anyway, she was outvoted and the family let me move into two rooms above the restaurant just until I got on my feet. So to speak."

"Why didn't your aunt want to help you? Isn't that what families are for?"

"Apparently not mine, but as I said, that's a long story. After my accident, when I was flat on my back in the hospital wondering if I'd ever walk again, well, that's what kept me going — my dream of having a business of my own, coming back to where my roots are. So," she says brightly, "now you know the whole sad story. Still interested?"

"I haven't heard anything to change my mind," I tell her, trying to be encouraging. She does have a license, I keep reminding myself. And she did work for Pinkerton's. "Everyone has . . . difficult periods. You're almost home free. When the insurance money arrives —"

"I'm not counting on that," she interrupts. "I can't keep living my life in the future. Postponing . . . what I want. I've been waiting for almost five months. So I'm just going ahead on my own, as if no money were ever coming to me. Trying to find a few small cases that I can manage." She smiles crookedly. "Maybe my ship will come in. But maybe it won't."

I'm a little embarrassed by all these revelations, but I guess she felt she had to let me know what I'm getting into. I give her full marks for honesty. "Coast Investigations," I say. "It sounds reassuring. Sensible. Better than the Trackers or the Wheelers."

"They're really okay, you know," she says. "And please, feel free to deal with them. As I said, I'm a damned good digger, and I do great phone interviews. But I haven't had any field experience. And now with my gimpy leg," she massages her knee, grimacing, "I'm not sure how well I can get around. What sort of case is this?" All business now, she takes a notebook out of her shirt pocket. "Let's hear about what you want me to do for you."

I take a deep breath, trying to collect my thoughts. Even though I'd rehearsed this at the harbor at Drizzle Bay, it still sounds ... dumb. Melodramatic. Ah, what the hell. I decide to just say it. "I think someone killed my aunt."

She looks at me, plainly startled.

"It's a complicated story," I say apologetically.

"That's okay," she says, trying to reassure me. "Just go ahead and tell it."

So I do, all of it. I tell her first of all about my dream, about remembering that Aunt Grace hated and feared the water, and then I tell Kerry how she was supposed to have died — snorkeling, for cripe's sake. Then I tell her about how damned evasive everyone at the B & B was, and about the scrap of conversation I'd overheard in the espresso bar. When I'm done, she says nothing for a few moments. Then she puts her notebook away. My heart sinks — she's decided not to take the case after all. Hell. I'll end up with the Trackers yet. "I have some questions I'd like to ask you," she says, "but unfortunately, I have to get back to work. What you've told me sounds . . . pretty serious all right."

"From what I've told you, do you think I'm . . . overreacting? I mean, murder is quite an accusation, I know, and —"

"I don't think it's overreacting to have the doubts you do. It does seem as though something pretty strange took place." She smiles and her eyes sparkle. I guess investigators get excited about this kind of thing — murder, I mean. "Let's talk again soon." She picks up her gun and jacket and we begin walking back to the casino. "Shall we? Talk again soon?"

I'm deep in thought and so the question comes as a surprise. "What? Oh. Yeah. We need to. But do we have, like, a deal? Do we need to do a contract?"

"Do you want to hire me? Remember, I told you I dig well, but I can't pound the pavement until my leg gets better."

"Yeah, I do want to hire you," I hear myself saying and I wonder if it's because she's impressed me with her professionalism, or because I feel sorry for her (guilt can be a wonderful persuader), or because she didn't laugh at my suspicions. Who's to know? "Do I have to sign something?"

She laughs. "No. Just give me a check. Then I'll get started."

I'm eager. "Well, what about when you get off work? We could figure out, you know, how to start, and I could pay you."

We're back at the front entrance to the gaming

center and I note that her frown is back in place. "Okay," she says. "I want to go home and change first. Take a shower, too. Why don't you meet me in the parking lot at the public dock. Just in front of the restaurant. We'll go somewhere and eat."

"What time?"

"Six-thirty?"

"Great." I'm so elated that I almost miss the little scene in front of the casino. Over to the right of the entrance, a couple of uniformed casino guards are gently propelling an intoxicated man in a floral shirt over to a bench in a clump of pines. Kerry sees them and the frown on her face turns to a look of hopelessness. Suddenly she looks like a seven-year-old swallowed up in a too-big uniform, a kid playing charades. She clearly senses me watching because she turns and gives me an embarrassed bitter smile, the hopelessness buried somewhere inside. *We all do what we have to,* her look seems to say. I hope, for her sake, that she doesn't have to do this much longer.

I spend the time between two and six-thirty in a little ocean wayside park, looking at the ocean, reading the local paper, and finally walking on the beach, wondering how everything was going to turn out. Replaying our conversation, I realize I'd neglected to tell Kerry that I was staying at the B & B incognito and when I do, I'm sure she'll tell me that was a pretty stupid thing to have done. I mean, how long did I think I could keep up the deception, anyhow? I'm getting depressed, I realize as I toss a stick of driftwood into the waves and resolve to try to talk myself into a better mood. I mean, I'm doing the right thing — getting an investigator to look at Aunt Grace's death — and who knows, maybe she'll find out that it really was an accident after all and the B & B folks are so evasive because they've been cooking the books (which is bad enough but not as bad as what I suspect) and that Delia and her cronies at the espresso bar were talking about nothing more serious than a solstice celebration. I mean, who knows what weird things go on here at the coast? I trudge up the sand a little farther and realize with a pang that one of the things wrong with me is that I'm homesick, for cripe's sake. As honky as it sounds, I miss Lancaster. Well, not exactly Lancaster, but I missed my cozy one-room apartment, my stacks of books, and most of all I miss Sam Spade, my cat. I decide that tonight I'd better call my cat-sitter Bradley, the gay guy who lives across the hall, and see how Sammy was doing. Not that Sammy would necessarily even care that I was gone — he adores Bradley and when I'm away, Brad lets Sammy pretty much rule the roost, feeding him tuna (albacore!), letting him shed his hair all over Brad's couch and sharpen his nails on the carpet. No wonder I couldn't get Mr. Spade to behave when I came home.

Not hurrying, I wander back to my car, take off my shoes and empty out the sand, and stare some more at the ocean. It certainly is pretty — dark blue sparkly water, powder blue sky, a few fluffy clouds. I could almost lapse into a fantasy about living here if it weren't for the specter of those mere 82 sunny days a year. I mean, how do people stand not seeing the sun for weeks and weeks? What do they do?

62

Awful Lancaster, smack in the middle of the Mojave Desert, midway between Los Angeles and Bakersfield, is one of the dustiest, dreariest, most depressing places I know — and while it wasn't my choice of places to live, I followed my army sergeant lover, Melanie, to Lancaster, and when she was posted to Germany, I just...stayed. When Mel's letters got shorter and less frequent, I passed from despair to depression to desuetude. Moving seemed too much effort and besides, why go anywhere else? What would change — I'd just take my baggage with me. So I stayed. In arid Lancaster, which suits me just fine. But at least the sun shines in Lancaster. I lace up my shoes, grab my backpack, and head to the bathroom to freshen up a little before my dinner with Kerry.

I pull into the parking lot at the Windsock public docks at about 6:25 and Kerry's there already, dressed in faded jeans and a white T-shirt. She's carrying a fawn suede bomber jacket and has her hair down. It's shorter than I thought — it falls to just about her jawline — and is as sleek and black as a raven's wing. Pretty darned attractive, I think as I pull up beside her and she smiles at me.

"You're punctual," I tell her, feeling a little confused because after all, I'm her employer — well, potential employer — and here I am having appreciative thoughts. She probably has a boyfriend, for cripe's sake, I remind myself as she climbs into the passenger seat of the Escort and buckles herself in.

"You're my future employer," she says as if she's read my thoughts. "It's up to me to impress you with my professionalism. Or something." She smiles again and I'm dazzled. Yikes.

"I'm willing to be impressed," I tell her. "Where is this going to take place?"

"Nautilus," she says. "There's an all-you-can-eat seafood buffet at one of the hotels. The dining room's a little noisy but they mostly leave you alone. I thought it would be a good place to talk business. Turn right out of the parking lot, then right again at 101 and keep going over the bridge into Nautilus. I'll direct you after that." She buckles herself in and tosses her jacket and cane into the backseat. "My check came," she tells me, smiling shyly.

"From . . . your insurance check? For your house? Really?"

"Yes," she says, the smile getting bigger, as pleased as Sammy the day he managed to bag a hummingbird. "There was a huge letter with the check — apparently everyone's been paid who needs to be paid and I have almost nine thousand dollars left over. Now I can look for someplace to rent, put a big down payment on a new car, and buy some clothes."

"And start Coast Investigations," I remind her quickly. I mean, someone has to be the sensible one here. I don't want my investigator off shopping, I want her with her nose to the ground, digging like a badger — her forté, as I recall.

"Sure," she says, looking at me reprovingly. "That's a given."

I relax. "Are you going to move?"

"You bet. I've told Daniel. He's not happy. And I called the gaming center and told my shift supervisor that I'd give the tribe two weeks' written notice tomorrow but he said not to bother. Can you imagine — they have people waiting in line for my job? He was a little huffy about my quitting — said that if he and my aunt hadn't been 'friends' I never would have gotten hired, and how lucky I was, blah, blah, blah. I'm going to send them a letter anyhow. I think it's good business practice. After all, they might want to use my professional services sometime in the future."

I'm getting nervous again. Already Kerry's making plans for the future — a future that I hope still includes me. But then she wouldn't be sitting here beside me taking me someplace where we could discuss business if she'd decided to dump me and my case, would she? I drive on, trying not to fret and pretty soon Kerry is directing me to turn right here and left there and shortly we're in the parking lot of a big gray hotel down by the Nautilus bayfront. I lock the Escort's door and catch Kerry walking a little taller, trying not to use her cane. She sees me looking and blushes.

"I'm starving," she says, to cover up.

"Me too," I tell her and reach to open the heavy front door for her.

"Oh," she says, plainly embarrassed. "Disabled red woman thanks you."

Now I'm embarrassed. "Um, you're welcome."

We find a table and when we're seated, Kerry looks over the top of her menu at me.

"You're frowning," she says. "Did I embarrass you? Was it the red woman part of what I said or the disabled part?"

"I guess . . . the red woman part. I mean, I don't know how I ought to feel about that."

She puts down her menu and looks at me gravely. "Well, how *do* you feel?"

"Mostly dumb. Because, I guess, I don't know how *you* feel about being, you know —"

"An Indian."

"Yeah. You see, I don't even know what to call you, for cripe's sake!"

"Okay," she says, "I guess we need to get this settled." She leans back in her chair. "I mostly try not to think too much about my heritage. I wasn't brought up in a tribal setting, the way most of us are. My mother . . . left the tribe and when she died, a white family raised me. I was only peripherally aware of Indian issues — they were something I read about in the newspaper. Then when I hit college, everything came crashing down on me — the students who were native rights advocates, the demonstrations. They tried pretty hard to recruit me and eventually one of them succeeded." She looks down at the table, smoothing the tablecloth nervously and I guess the "one of them" was a lover. "Anyhow," she continues, "all that passion, all that involvement, only got me one thing — kicked out of University of Washington's law school. I lost my scholarship." She looks up quickly to see how I was taking this. "Yeah, dumb, right? So I got my head screwed on straight, found a two-year college with a criminal justice program, and got a crummy certificate instead of the degree I wanted." She slumped a little in her chair. "To say

I'm ambivalent about being an Indian would be an understatement. So my confusion and bitterness just . . . pops out sometimes in my Indian jokes." She looked up, a rueful smile on her face. "Sorry."

"It's okay," I tell her, touched by her confession. "I understand better now." So I decide to entrust her with a confidence of my own. "Being a member of a minority group is a bummer."

Kerry looks at me quickly, wondering, I'm sure, what kind of minority group I could possibly belong to. The sisterhood of garnet-haired, tattooed, Californian female weirdos? "I'm gay," I tell her grimly. "We don't have a heritage to feel ambivalent about."

The appearance of a waiter precludes any more confessions and I'm just as happy. We'll be crying on each other's shoulders soon, for cripe's sake.

The waiter, a young guy in his 20's, deposits water and a basket of bread on our table, smiling. The smile kind of fades a little as Kerry looks up at him, and I find myself getting angry on her behalf. Fortunately, she doesn't notice. Or at least I think she doesn't. "We'll both have the seafood buffet," she tells him. "I'd like a beer, too. A Rogue Red. Allison?"

"Okay, sure," I answer, distracted. "Sounds good." The waiter leaves us in peace.

"A scholarship to law school," I say in genuine admiration. "That's quite an accomplishment."

"Yeah, I guess so. And that's another thing I feel . . . guilty about."

"Guilty? About losing your scholarship?"

"No. About getting it in the first place."

"I don't understand."

"Well, chances are if I'd had a normal tribal childhood, I wouldn't have finished school or gone to college or done anything. But I didn't have a normal childhood." She grimaces. "My mother was an Indian — an Owyhee — but my dad was white. From Alaska. An oilfield worker. I don't know how they met — the cousins won't tell me. Anyhow, he got her pregnant they disappeared and before anyone knew it, they were living in Alaska. Then he was killed in a drilling platform accident, leaving her alone and ineligible for any of his benefits and she got sick and died of pneumonia. Child Protective Services had me in a foster home faster than you can say Pocahontas and that's where I stayed." She grimaces again. "No one on my mother's side of the family wanted to take me in — I guess her sister in particular was pretty disgusted with her for what she did. And CPS was very reluctant to let me go back to Oregon. So I grew up in Alaska with a nice white, middle-class family. I had a dog, a bike, a paper route — the whole thing. And they encouraged me to be good in school, so I was. What they didn't do, though — wouldn't do — was to let me learn anything about my culture. They thought it would only bring me grief." She shrugged. "So here I am — the best-educated and the dumbest person in my tribe. A white Indian."

I think about this. "Do you want to learn — about your tribe? About being an Indian?"

"Yeah. I do. I didn't always, but I do now. I'm tired of being ignorant and I'm tired of having people be my backstop. I think I'm old enough to handle trouble. And smart enough to navigate my way to who I am." She held up her beer bottle and looked at it in mock surprise. "Gee — give me one beer and I tell you my life story. Sorry, Allison."

"No problem," I say and mean it.

"Let's get some food," she says. "I'm starved."

I trail thoughtfully along to the buffet table, so laden with fishy offerings it's almost groaning. Kerry takes a whole plate of crab legs and nothing else and I decide to sample a little of this and a little of that — a salmon the size of a beagle baked in a lemon and butter sauce, crèpes filled with scallops, cheese and spinach, broiled halibut skewered with vegetables, and a couple of enormous baked oysters. Our waiter had brought our beer and salads so we dig in, eating and murmuring.

"I love these crab legs," Kerry explains as she puts away her eighth. "And they go fast."

I polish off my plate of food and find, amazingly, that my spirits have lifted about fifty percent. The Rogue ale isn't exactly dampening my outlook on things either, so we order another beer and gird our loins for a return to the buffet table. I'm more selective this time, limiting myself to a couple of crab claws, a small piece of salmon, and another halibut-on-a-stick thingie.

After a while, we're sated. "So, let's talk business," she says. "Tell me exactly what you'd like me to do for you."

I've thought about this, so the answer is easy. "Find out how my aunt really died."

She shreds the label on her beer bottle. "So you don't think she drowned?"

"Oh, I think she drowned all right. I also think she might have had help." I can hardly believe I'm saying this but now that I hear the words spoken out loud, they're not so bad.

Kerry winces. "You're talking about murder. That's a pretty serious accusation."

"I know that. But I don't think there's any way she was snorkeling, got tired or dizzy or disoriented or whatever, and went down for the count. Like I told you, Aunt Grace wasn't a swimmer."

"So what was she doing out there at the rocks on a boat?"

"I don't know. But I do know — no, scratch that — I believe that the four women I saw Delia with were involved in all this."

"Yeah? Maybe."

I bristled. "Maybe."

"Yeah. Maybe. There could be a simple explanation. They may just be, you know, grieving."

I give Kerry a glare. "Hey, whose side are you on here?"

"You may not like this, and it may sound corny, but I'm on the side of truth. If we agree to do business, that's what I'll be searching for. The truth."

I stifle the urge to say something smart and instead consider this statement. The truth. Well, isn't that what I want, too — to learn the truth? "I guess that's what I want to know," I said. "I want to know what Aunt Grace was doing out there in the ocean, what part the four women in the espresso bar had to play in her death, and what the crazy ladies at the Bed and Breakfast know that's making them spooky. I want to know why Aunt Grace left each of them ten grand. And there may be some more things I want to know as we go along. Does that all fall under the umbrella of the truth?"

Kerry considers this. "When we find the truth, we'll probably know the answers to those questions. Everything seems to be tied together." She looks at me levelly. "Okay. I'll take your case. Write me a check for five hundred dollars and I'll get started tomorrow."

I dig in my backpack, not willing to give her a chance to change her mind. "Thanks," I say. Then: "Do I make the check out to you or to Coast Investigations?"

She grins. "I'll have to go open a business account to cash it, but go ahead and make it to Coast Investigations." I hand her the check and she looks at it for so long that I wonder if I've made a spelling mistake.

"Something wrong?"

"Nope. I was just thinking that it's been quite a day."

There's a couple of swallows of beer left in my glass and I hold it up. "Here's to you. And to what your insurance money will make possible. And to Coast Investigations." And to finding out what I want to know, I add mentally. We clink glasses and I can't help asking, "So how does an investigation start? What will you do first?"

"Rent an office. Get a phone installed. Buy a fax. Get a computer and a modem. Hook them up."

"Why so high-tech? Can't you just, you know, go ask questions?"

"Asking questions is useful, but it's only a part of an investigation. The day of the gumshoe is over.

Besides, as I explained, I'm not an interrogator, I'm a —"

"A digger. I remember."

"Right. So if all goes well, I'll have a copy of the medical examiner's report and the death certificate by noon. By the way, I'll want you to sign a power of attorney giving me the authority to act for you in these matters. Next, if there was a will, it will have been probated. The proceedings of probate court are a matter of public record. We'll start with those things."

I'm impressed. And encouraged. I guess she does know how to dig. "Okay. What can I do in the meantime?"

"You? Don't spook those women at Lavner Bay. I'll want to talk to them. So pack a lunch. Go away for the day."

"And do what? I don't know a soul here. And besides, I'm too agitated to play tourist."

"Well, come and help me. Like I said, I'm going to rent space tomorrow and buy business equipment. And maybe a few clothes."

"Oh no you don't," I tell her. "No clothes shopping on my time." But this may not be such a bad idea. After all, if I'm keeping an eye on her, she'll have to be ferreting out the truth, not restocking her wardrobe. Or buying fast cars. "Okay," I say. "Tell me when and where."

"Nine in the morning. At the crabbing dock. The parking lot."

I should have known. "I'll be there," I tell her.

Chapter 6

It's after ten and the B & B is dark and quiet,
buttoned up as tight as a ... let's just say it's
buttoned up tight. I unlock the front door and slip
inside, feeling like a cat burglar, and the feeling
makes me angry. Hey, I haven't done anything
wrong. Well, maybe I'm guilty of a little deception,
but that's all. I try not to make a sound as I climb
the stairs to my room and when I'm safely inside,
my backpack on the bed, the door locked behind me,
I realize that I've been holding my breath. Nuts to
this, I think as I snap on the light, make a circuit of

the room, and then flop on the bed, my brain buzzing from everything that's happened.

I ought to feel more encouraged — heck, I've got an ex-Pinkerton's investigator working for me but the only emotion I can identify is anxiety. A quick phone call to Bradley in Lancaster confirms that Sammy is doing just fine without me. So much for feeling needed. Now I have depression to add to my anxiety.

For some reason, the image of Kerry's aunt and cousins in the seafood restaurant come to my mind. Heck, Kerry has a cast of thousands for a family — a whole *tribe,* for cripe's sake. They may not approve of what she's doing, but they got her a job at the gaming center and are giving her a place to live. I have to admit it — I'm envious. What would a big family feel like? Several other unworthy thoughts suggest themselves to me — she's almost a lawyer, she's gorgeous, she has money — but I stuff them back into their slimy lair. Life isn't a bowl of cherries for Kerry — she almost bought the big one in that fire in Portland, she may never walk right again, she isn't exactly her aunt's favorite niece. Still, there's the seductive thought of that big family in the background. And her tribe. She'll figure out how she fits into it. Whereas I, where do I fit? There's no big family in my background, and no heritage for me to claim. I have a moment of panic — is this what it means to be a lesbian? Never to have a family? Never to be a member of a community? To have a partner, maybe, if you're lucky, but essentially to be alone, unconnected to any group bigger than your little unit of two? Crap, I don't even have a lover. Instead, I have . . . what? Only a cat. Who's getting along fine without me. *Pretty fucking pathetic,* I mutter.

To distract myself from self-pity, I get up and pace. Thinking about family has brought me back to the problem of Aunt Grace and what the hell happened to her and I realize with a jolt that she must have left behind . . . things. Personal effects. Clothes. Papers. Maybe even a journal. Why didn't the lawyer mention these things to me? For that matter, where the hell are they? Here, at the B & B? Why not — isn't it logical that Aunt Grace would have lived here? Why didn't I ask someone — Pan, Delia, anyone — if my aunt had lived here? Maybe I can find that out tomorrow. Even this small, concrete chore makes me feel a little better.

I turn off the light, pace over to the window, and pull up the shade. The sea looks like a piece of rippled black silk. Overhead a thin crescent moon gives just enough light to make everything other-worldly. The little beach I can see from my window could be spilled sugar, it looks so white. The scene looks so alien that I shiver — I mean, I'm used to looking outside at home and seeing the so-called garden apartments across from mine. Something solid. Not this huge . . . emptiness. What the hell am I *doing* here, I ask myself. And not for the first time, either. Then I amend my question. I really know what I'm doing here, so that's not exactly it. My complaint is more of a metaphysical one. Maybe a cosmic *Why?* would be more appropriate. Why me, why now, why this?

I never have done well with sudden, unplanned change. It makes me feel displaced and powerless and that makes me crazy. Back home I've arranged my life so I'm in control. I have a small life, with a short list of have-to's and minuscule expectations of myself. But I have a life I can handle. I have order because I've created it. Now, suddenly, everything's been turned upside down. I feel as though I'm buried under a huge, tangled ball of wool. I feel as if I'm smothering.

Get a grip, I say and close my eyes, pressing my forehead to the glass. My glass, I remind myself. My window. My bed and breakfast. My new business. *Run. Run away. Run fast,* a scared little voice inside me says. *You don't have to take care of this. Leave the damned B & B to those crazy women.* And I would, I realize, I would run. If it weren't for Aunt Grace. Along with the B & B I seem to have inherited a problem. The problem of what really happened to my aunt. And I can't run from that. She plunged into the surf to find me; I can damned well wade into this morass and find her. Well, can't I? Surely, with Kerry's help I can.

Once before I pulled the tatters of my life around me and made a whole thing of them — presumably I can do it again. After all, I'm older now and presumably smarter. *But there are an awful lot of tatters this time,* that scared little inner voice tells me. *An awful lot.* Yeah, I say back, there are. There sure are.

Chapter 7

As usual, Kerry's right on time. Still smiling, too. Must be the prospect of our shopping expedition.

"Have a muffin," I offer. "There was a basket of them on the breakfast table at the B & B. I grabbed a few and a couple bananas as I ran out the door."

"Thanks," she says. "Let's get some coffee at the espresso hut in town. Make a left at the light and you'll see it on the left. It's one of those drive-through places. They have great coffee."

We get a couple of lattes and I'm just about to pull onto 101. "Where now?" I want to know.

"Turn left," she says. "Toward Lavner Bay. There's an out-of-business motel at the top of the hill that I want to take a look at. Early this morning I contacted the real estate firm that's handling the property. Someone's going to meet me there."

I'm skeptical. An out-of-business motel? Sounds pricey. But what the heck, it's Kerry's money she's spending, so I eat my muffin, drink my coffee, and drive. Sure enough, at the top of a little hill, set back from the road, is a collection of four little cabins connected by breezeways and a larger structure — presumably the manager's cottage. It's a whole lot cuter than I imagined and even has a coat of new blue paint. There's a white Plymouth Voyager in the driveway and a handsome woman of about 50, short gray hair combed carefully back from her face, navy pants, white polo shirt and a brocade vest, clipboard in hand, is standing outside, drinking from a paper coffee cup and admiring the day. Another java head, I see.

I get out with Kerry — what the heck, the sun's shining — and I see the real estate agent do a double take as we approach. I look at Kerry who seems pretty conservatively dressed — khaki pants, a crisp yellow Oxford cloth shirt — and then I realize that it's me who's freaking the agent out. Not for the first time since arriving here I feel . . . inadequate. I guess my hair, my pierced eyebrow, and my ripped jeans and oversized, faded black T-shirt is just not appropriate attire here on the coast. I've been spoiled. In Lancaster, I didn't have to stir out of my apartment to do my business so I just got in the habit of dressing the same for every occasion. Well, I did have to take packages of books to the post office, but everyone's so catatonic there they wouldn't have noticed if I'd come in wearing a body bag. Or nothing. I hope the agent's alarm won't translate into higher rent for Kerry. Or no deal. I want my investigator to be able to investigate, for cripe's sake.

"Hi," the agent says, recovering nicely.

"I'm Kerry Owyhee," Kerry says forthrightly, extending her hand. They shake, and the agent smiles. "This is Allison O'Neil, a friend." The agent extends her hand to me with markedly less enthusiasm and I find myself relieved that I'm right and that it's me she disapproves of, not Kerry.

"I'm Jaimie Hastings," she says.

"Hi," Kerry says. "I'd like to take a look at this property. As I told you on the phone, right now I'm interested in renting. Later, if I like it, I might be interested in purchasing."

"You mentioned that you're an investigator," Jaimie said with what seemed to be genuine interest, and I wander off, leaving the two of them to it. The four little cabins seem sturdy and well-built and I see that the breezeways which attach them together are really carports, with room for woodpiles. I walk through one of the carports to the rear of the property. Every unit has its own fenced patio, with a little gate leading to a small clearing at the rear of the property. I walk across the clearing to a thicket of blackberry bushes that loom higher than I can reach. Off to one side, there's a narrow path that bisects the thicket and I note with curiosity that it seems pretty well-used. It's barely as wide as my shoulders, but I take a few steps onto the path, then a few more. Pretty soon I'm feeling like Alice in Wonderland as the berry vines almost close on me overhead, leaving me in what seems to be a tunnel. I'm a little spooked, so I stop, look around and then down, and to my astonishment in the damp earth are the prints of . . . what? I bend down for a better look. Sharp feet. Scratch that — these are hoof prints. As in deer. Many hooves. And other prints I can't recognize, made by long, skinny toes. Awed, I realize this must be an animal trail. I swallow nervously, imagining many brown eyes watching, and mutter, "It's okay guys, I'm a friend," like they could understand, for cripe's sake. Then I turn and carefully retrace my steps.

Soon I'm back in the sun behind the second cabin and I look at the berry vines more carefully. Just as I thought, a short distance behind the vines is the ever-present forest. I guess the critters live in the woods and come down the trail to do what — eat the berries? Visit with the guests? What a kick. And then I think about Lorien at the B & B. My B & B. There's no forest there — either it doesn't grow on the clifftops or it was cut to permit building, so someone must have planted a grove. A wild place. A forest heart. This thought touches me in a way I haven't been touched in years and I sit down on a stump and look around.

There's a clump of orange bell-like flowers with long, slender leaves and I realize I have no idea what their name is. Or for that matter, what the trees are called. Each one is different. One is tall and dense with stiff, short, blue needles, one is slender and supple with broad, feathery needles and limber branches, and there's one whose needles are long and bright green. I feel panicked. Do I know *anything*?

Out of nowhere a fat grasshopper lands on my

shirt and I carefully pluck her off and put her in my palm and look at her. There she sits moving her jaws back and forth instead of up and down, gazing around with her enormous and complicated eyes, washing her face with her forearms. Now she snaps her wings open and floats away, defying gravity. I realize with a pang of loss that I haven't *seen* a grasshopper in years let alone held one in my hand. I close my eyes. Didn't I do this all the time when I was a kid — find a field, fall down in the grass, study the bugs, then roll over and watch the clouds? What happened to me? What happens to any of us?

"There you are," says Kerry, her Topsiders crunching on the gravel of the carport.

"Here I am," I reply, coming back to this reality of rentals and business deals and, heaven help us all, murder investigations. "So, are you going to rent the place?"

She nods. "Yeah. I got it for a song."

"I wonder why." I think protectively of the animal trail and the scrap of forest where the wild things are and wonder if I should tell her. I decide not to. "How did you come to pick out this particular place?" I ask.

"I've noticed it as I drive back and forth," she says. "It's always appealed to me. I drove in once and had a look around and it seemed to me — I know this will sound crazy — it seemed to me that I remembered it."

"Oh yeah? I thought you were born in Alaska?"

"I was. So I can't think why this place should be familiar. I mean, I can't have been here."

"Maybe you were," I tell her. "Maybe when you were a kid, your foster family brought you here to —

I don't know — meet your tribe. Get in touch with your roots."

She shook her head. "Not the Wyfords. That's my foster family's name — Wyford. Not them. It would have had to be before that. When I lived in a kids' group home in Ketchikan. But I was pretty young then — not even three." She shook her head. "Or maybe I only think I remember it."

"So, when can you move in?"

"Today. Now." She held up the key. "So we'd better get busy."

I agree. I can't wait to get her installed and working. "What's next?"

"Business equipment. Then a car. Clothes can wait. I've got a few. I want to set up my office in the main house and get everything hooked up. Jaimie's going to get the power and phone turned on for me. So let's go. There's an electronics store in Nautilus that will have what I want. I'd rather go to Eugene, but we're pressed for time, right?"

"Right," I say sternly.

At the end of an hour, we're stuffing a brand-new Pentium computer into the back seat of the Escort and finding space in the trunk for a monitor, a printer, a fax, a modem, a box of printer paper, assorted cables and wires, and a few other boxed goodies I've lost track of. The bill is well over $5,000 but Kerry writes a check without turning a hair. My admiration for her is growing by the minute — I mean, she must actually know how all this electronic stuff fits together. I, on the other hand, had trouble getting my answering machine hooked up.

On our way back to Waldport, we pass the Toyota dealership and Kerry says, "Hey, turn around, please. I'll just be a minute." So I U-turn on the highway — an act that produces great honking of horns — and wheel into the Toyota lot. "I'll only be ten minutes. I promise," Kerry says, and I believe her. I barely have time to settle down and begin reading the *Nautilus Times* when she's back.

"Done?" I ask.

"Done. I can pick it up about five."

"Pick what up?"

"My car. Truck, rather. I just bought a Toyota Tacoma. I love Toyotas — no dickering about extras. All you have to pick is the color."

I'm amazed. "And yours is?"

"Red."

I wonder if this is another Indian joke but say nothing. "So, back to the . . . whatever it is you've rented. What should I call it by the way?"

"Good question. How about my office."

I pull out onto the highway. "What are you going to do with the other buildings — the cabins?"

Kerry shrugs. "I haven't a clue. Maybe I'll rent them to tourists. Maybe I'll sub-lease them to small businesses. I haven't had time to think much about it."

I help Kerry tote all the boxes of electronics stuff into the big cabin's main room where we deposit everything on the floor. Kerry starts right to work, unpacking things, tossing empty boxes and styrofoam into the corner and I suddenly realize that I'm superfluous here.

"Do you need any help with this?" I offer lamely.

"What?" she says, looking up hands full of wires and cords. "No, I don't think so. It's going to take me about an hour to get everything up and running." She plugs a phone wire into the jack — "Great!" — then disconnects it and plugs it into her fax. "Darn," she says, looking around. "What I do need is a phone book. And I really could use a couple of tables. Do you think . . ."

"Yeah, I could get them," I offer, realizing I'm actually pleased to be useful.

She peels a check out of her checkbook, signs it, and gives it to me. "Maybe three six-foot tables. And a couple of office chairs. Oh, and a desk if you see one that's not too expensive. There's an office furniture place opposite the post office. They deliver, although if you could get one table into the Escort, it'd help a lot. And the phone company is on Willow Street, just east of 101."

I've left Kerry with her one table — the furniture store is delivering the other stuff this afternoon — and I'm now cruising down the hill to town. I'm too antsy to stick around and watch Miss O play connect the wires; I have to do something. Besides, I have ideas of my own regarding how an investigation ought to proceed — I sell mystery novels, right? And I've read every one — especially the Caitlin Reece series. If I've learned anything, it's that P.I.s get out there and beat the pavement. So while Miss O is stringing wires, I'm going to do some sleuthing of my own.

The Daily Grind is only a hop and a skip away from Kerry's new digs, so it takes me about thirty-eight seconds to get there. I leave the Escort at the little state park, admire the bay, the bridge, and the view, and amble across the street to the coffee-house. Most of the patrons are out on the deck soaking up some rays, but I buy my latte and sit inside where I can make eye contact with the *barista*. As I had hoped, the same young lady is on duty who was working the other day when I saw Delia and her cronies. And maybe, just maybe, I can get her talking. I mean, this is what real P.I.s do — pump folks for information. We'll see just how successful I am.

"Hi," I say after she's served another foursome bound for the deck. She gives me a smile that turns into a look of recognition, and I'm flattered that she remembers me. I mean, who could forget a face like mine, right? Ha. Most likely it's the hair she remembers, and most likely she remembers that because it's the same hue as hers, only hers is shorter and spikier. Today she's wearing an olive green T-shirt that says Java Head, a long black cotton skirt, and Doc Martens. A name tag pinned to her shirt says Dee. "Gorgeous day, isn't it?" I offer as a conversation starter.

"Yeah," she says. "Summer's like this — sunshine day after day. You should see fall and winter, though."

"Lots of rain?"

"Well, yeah, it rains a lot. But the wind!" She

makes a face. "Last December twelfth we had this storm that was *so* bad! I mean, I lost my electricity for a day but lots of people lost theirs for a week! And we had trees down all over the place. God, they fell right on people's houses in the middle of the rain and everything! The wind was clocked at one-fourteen in Nautilus. Blew the roof right off a restaurant."

"Wow," I commiserate. "Sounds bad."

"It was horrible," she says, coming out from behind the counter and swiping at a tabletop. "As soon as I save some money, I'm going to, like, Nevada. Someplace where they don't have a coast."

"Oh yeah? And here I was thinking of moving here," I say, slipping into yet another fantasy role — State-Changing Job-Seeker this time. Sometimes I scare myself when I assume these roles — like I might get stuck inside the persona I've created and not be able to find my way back to the real me. Whoever that is.

"I've probably scared you off, haven't I?" she says, contrite. "But not every winter is as bad as last winter. Really. Sometimes we're out on the beach in our T-shirts in February."

Sure you are. T-shirts and six sweaters, I think. "No, you haven't scared me off. The lack of jobs might scare me off, though. This is a pretty small town. There's probably not much work."

"Oh, there are more jobs than you'd think," she says, ambling back behind the counter to clean a little more. "All the businesses in town need help from time to time."

"I worked in a B & B in California," I say inventively. "I was thinking of looking around for that kind of job."

She wrinkles her nose. "What — cleaning motel rooms?"

"Not exactly. You know — checking people in, making up the rooms, getting breakfast ready. In exchange for room and board."

She nods. "I get it. But most B & B owners around here live on the premises and do the work themselves."

"Too bad," I say. Then, as though the thought had just occurred to me: "What about Lavner Bay? I hear the owner just died."

"Uh huh. They might need someone."

"I know a girl who stayed there for a while," my persona says. "She told me they're an awfully strange bunch."

"Oh yeah?" She looks up from cleaning her espresso machine. "They're always nice enough when they come in here. Is your friend, you know, a regular person?"

"A regular person?" As opposed to what, a decaf person? What a question!

"Yeah, a regular person. You know, straight."

"Er, well —"

"It's okay to be gay," she tells me, a smile of amusement on her lips. "It seems like half the people in town are." She points to a sign on the wall: HATE-FREE ZONE. DEGRADING OR INSULTING ETHNIC, RACIAL, OR SEXUAL REMARKS NOT WELCOME IN THIS ESTABLISHMENT. "A lot of the gay or gay-friendly businesses in town have one of these. We mean it, too."

I remember what Bree told me about the vast sisterhood of Lavner Bay and as I remember, an amazing thought hits me. "Lavner Bay has one of those signs. Right by the check-in counter. But the owner, Grace O'Neil ... I mean, she isn't, er, wasn't ... was she?"

"I don't know," the kid says matter-of-factly. "Probably. Why, what's the matter? You don't want to work for them now that you've found out they're all lesbians?"

I laugh out loud. "No. It's not that. It's just that I'm, well, I'm stunned." *Aunt Grace? A lesbian?* I laugh again.

"Yeah, it is kind of amazing, isn't it? All these *women.* They just kind of gravitate to the coast. Do you think this is a nexus?" she asks.

"A what?"

"A nexus. A female energy convergence point. You know, like Back O' Beyond, in Arizona."

She's lost me, but I consider it wise to agree. "Could be." But I want to get back to a more interesting topic. "Cordelia and Grace, at Lavner Bay, do you think they were, like —"

She shakes her head. "Lovers? I don't know. Grace was a very spiritual person. That's not to say that spiritual people don't have lovers, but I don't think Grace did. She was, like, on another level. She and Cordelia and four or five other women used to meet here every Sunday morning for what they called church." She laughed. "They'd meet on the deck, read poetry, talk, laugh. Like that."

I feel a sudden stab of envy. This coffee-slinging kid knew more about my aunt than I ever would. But I stifle my envy long enough to register her comment about the four or five other women. "I think I met them the other night at the B & B," I fib. "Were they Jaimie Hastings and her friends?"

Dee shakes her head. "No. Let's see, there was Delia and Grace, Mary White and Whitney, Paula Eyde, and Robin what's-her-name who has that counseling and herbal business down by the dock."

I silently repeated the names to myself. "Oh," I say blandly. "Must be a different group."

"You seem to know Cordelia and Grace," Dee says, curious.

"Um, no. My friend did. She talked a lot about them. So I feel I know them too."

"Too bad you missed the memorial service," she says. "It was Sunday. They were all there."

"I'm sorry, too," I say honestly. A couple of tourists come up to the counter and Dee turns her attention to them, taking their order and disappearing for a moment. I wander over to the bulletin board and read the business cards just for something to do, when all of a sudden, a lavender card catches my eye: *The Metamorphosis Center, Robin Myers — Healing Arts Practitioner and Herbalist, Sacred Rituals Taught and Performed*. Chances are this is the Robin of Aunt Grace's group. Glancing around furtively, I unpin her card, stuff it in my pocket, and scuttle out the door, muttering to myself the names of the women like a mantra.

Once in the Escort, I scrabble in my backpack for a piece of paper, then write down the names of Grace and Delia's friends. What a gold mine Dee has proven to be, the little blabbermouth. I hold Robin's card up in front of me, laughing when I see that her house or office or studio or whatever is practically beside the Coast Seafood Restaurant. Do I dare just walk in and start talking? Kerry told me not to spook them, to stay away, but I can be clever and careful. Heck, investigators in the books I sell do this sort of thing all the time. *Yeah, but you're not the investigator — Kerry is,* my inner voice says. *What's in a name,* I ask it with more bravado than I feel. This is my lead. I found it and I'm going to follow up on it. Besides, what would Kerry do if I gave it to her — feed it into her computer? My stomach does a little flip-flop because I sense I'm really on the trail now, and quick, before I lose my nerve, I start the Escort and drive off.

Chapter 8

The Metamorphosis Center is a bright yellow house three down from the Coast Seafood Restaurant. There are plenty of crab ring renters today and I cruise the parking lot, finally getting a space at the far end. A white picket fence encloses the Center's yard and inside is a flower garden with big gray-green bushes that my nose tells me are lavender. A fat orange cat is asleep on the porch and I have to step over him to get to the front door, which is open.

"Hi!" I call, but no one answers. I take the plunge and go inside. Incense is burning somewhere — there's a tangy, aromatic smell in the air — and the front room is so cheerful and full of sun that it makes me want to smile. Or stay awhile. The orange cat has followed me inside and hops up on one of the wicker chairs, arranging himself decoratively against the multi-colored pillows. Someone who loves light and color and life lives here and I feel guilty for perpetrating yet another deception. There are copies of *Vegetarian Life* on a little table, and I pick one up and leaf through it while I'm waiting. I'm deep into an article on mushrooms, when a door closes somewhere inside and I hear footsteps. The cat jumps down, uttering happy trilling sounds, and a woman comes into the room, her arms full of flowers. She's the woman from the espresso bar, the one who was hugging Delia, the lady with the salt-and-pepper hair.

"I thought I heard someone come in," she says, "but I had my hands full. I'm so glad you waited. I'm Robin. Let me just put these down out here." I hear her rustling around in the kitchen. "Tea?" she calls. "I was just about to have some."

"Oh, er, sure," I call. Then, remembering my manners: "Thank you."

"So," the woman says, coming to rejoin me, the cat in her arms. "What brings you here on such a beautiful day?"

I suddenly decide that I can't do this. Maybe Kerry or my fictional investigators would have no problem grilling this gentle, earnest soul, but I do. Dammit. Besides, what this woman does is too close to what I need — a metamorphosis from my anxiety, guilt, depression, and anger. "Um, er," I stammer, sounding like an idiot.

"Let's have some tea," she says, "and I'll tell you what we do here. Why don't you come into the kitchen with me while I make it. Would you like to carry Amberilla?" She hands me the cat.

"I'd absolutely, positively love to carry Amberilla," I tell her, taking the fat feline and burying my face in her fur. The cat sings on an ascending note and for some reason, I feel like crying.

I sit at a small cobalt blue kitchen table, on a red chair with an enormous yellow poppy painted on the seat. "Ginseng tea?" Robin asks and although I've never had ginseng in my life, I willingly agree. She hands me a steaming mug and as I take it, she says, "Why, you're sad. Aren't you?"

I look up in amazement. "I hadn't thought so," I tell her. "But now that you mention it, yes, I am." It seems harmless enough to admit this, and who knows, it might provide me with a circular path back to what I really want to talk about — the circumstances surrounding my aunt's death.

"Are you grieving for someone?"

This woman's perceptiveness astounds me. "I . . . a member of my family just died. I hadn't seen her for years, but now I realize that she probably loved me a lot. I wish I'd stayed in touch." I don't know if this qualifies as grieving, but it's a conversation starter, anyhow.

Robin nods, cradling her mug of tea in two hands. "Feelings about death are . . . hard," she says. "If you want to work through your grief, you have to be prepared to go on a journey."

I've read about the different stages of grieving, so I guess this is what she's talking about. "Could you help me?"

93

"Possibly," she says, studying my face. She frowns a little and I know what she's going to say before she says it. "Do I know you?"

I shake my head. "I've never met you before. In fact, I've never been to Oregon before."

"Still, I have the strangest feeling . . ."

"How much would you charge?" I ask, wanting to scuttle this line of thought.

"Oh, well, I have a sliding scale. Anywhere from fifteen to fifty dollars an hour. You decide where you fit on the scale."

I nod. "And we would, what, talk?"

"Mostly."

I decide to take the plunge. Watching her closely, I say, "My relative, this person who died, well I think she may have had . . . help."

Robin's eyes open in alarm. "Help? What kind of help?"

"Well, I just don't see how she could have died by accident the way everyone tells me she did, and she was healthy so there's no way she would have committed suicide, so that only leaves one other explanation." Robin makes a choking sound and raises a hand to her throat. "I think she may have been, well, um, killed. Possibly . . ."

Robin's in such a state of alarm that I trail off. Either I've hit the nail on the head or she's still grieving for Aunt Grace herself and this whole scenario has hit too close to home. Dammit. Do professional investigators run into these dilemmas — the many-branched tree of explanations? How the hell do they ever sort anything out? And of course her alarm makes me feel guiltier still — she's a nice person and here I am, ruining her tranquillity. I can't win.

"Perhaps you shouldn't be talking to me," Robin says weakly. "Perhaps you should be talking to the police."

"I intend to," I tell her. "Just as soon as I get back to California. I just got the news. I'm on . . . vacation," I say, mixing truth with lies.

She relaxes visibly and I know that I'm onto something. The only problem is, I don't know what.

"You should probably seek the services of someone like me when you get home," she says. "The transformation process I spoke of would probably take many weeks."

"Oh," I say. "Okay." This seems the appropriate time to conclude our meeting, so I finish my tea. Standing up, I scoop Amberilla up in my arms and walk to the front door. Robin walks with me. "Thanks for talking to me. And for the tea. And letting me hug Amberilla." I look back into the cheerful front room and what I can see of the kitchen. Amberilla closes her eyes and leans her head against my shoulder.

"You're welcome," Robin says, looking at me with concern and I know, I just *know,* that whatever this woman is guilty of — and, dammit, she's guilty of something — it isn't murder.

Eyde Gallery is a neat, one-story, white-painted brick structure just outside Windsock on the road to Nautilus. There are three other cars in the lot and I pull up beside one of them and sit for a moment, preparing to don a new persona. But nothing occurs to me and I realize it's because I'm bummed out, really bummed out. To tell the truth, I'm ashamed of the fact that I alarmed Robin. Worse than that, I'm distressed because in another lifetime, I might have wanted her for a friend, or at least a confidant. I'm amazed that I'm thinking this because I've never really had women friends, not after I got out of school. And even then, it seemed that the only interest I had in other women was as potential bed partners. Call it shallow, call it overly libidinous, call it what you want but that's the way it was. Which meant that I never had friends, not real friends. Only past, present, and potential lovers. Therefore, realizing that I might be interested in another woman as a friend and not a bed partner sort of blows me away, and I sit in the Escort, wondering what on earth is happening to me. Could I be undergoing (I hate even to think the word after disgracing myself at Robin's) a metamorphosis? A sea change? Somehow here on the coast where things are green and growing and people actually seem happy to be here, the possibility that I might be changing doesn't seem as ridiculous as it would were I back in Lancaster where nothing ever changes. I mean we don't even have *seasons,* for cripe's sake. I turn the idea over in my mind and it kind of excites me. After all, everything changes, so why not me? God knows I haven't been deliriously happy with my life in California.

One of the coast's ubiquitous ravens plops down on the gravel beside my car and eyes me inscrutably.

"Well?" I ask him, getting out of the Escort and closing the door gently so as not to scare him.

"Cawwwk," he opines unhelpfully, looking at me with bright black eyes. I crunch down the gravel path to the gallery and open the door.

Fortunately there are half a dozen other people wandering around and browsing, so I'm able to sidle past the owner (the dark-haired woman with glasses I saw at the coffeeshop — Paula Eyde, I presume) and disappear temporarily into a back corner of the gallery to plan my strategy. I pass a display of gorgeous shimmering blue raku pots, some terrific soapstone carvings, a dozen or so handmade paper landscapes, and realize in amazed horror that I haven't set foot in an art gallery in over eight years. Not since I got out of school, came to Lancaster to be with Melanie, and beached myself there like a disoriented dolphin when she left me. During the four years that I've been imitating a mole, artists have been creating beauty like this to speak directly to souls like mine, but I somehow missed the message. Missed it? Ha — I haven't even been listening. So, I'm knocked out thinking about all this, when I turn around and see my aunt.

My heart almost leaps out of my mouth and I lurch backward into the raku, knocking a pot off its stand with my elbow, sending it to the floor with what sounds like a very expensive crash. But that's the least of my worries because seriously, for maybe six or seven heartbeats, I think either I'm losing my mind or else all this has been a very bad dream and my aunt is here in front of me. And then I realize I'm looking at a photograph. And what a photograph.

Hell, my aunt looks *alive*. The image is life-sized and it's my aunt looking head on at the camera, leaning against a windowsill, and it's all so real you think maybe she's going to speak to you. The window is framed in green curtains and there's a vase of bright yellow daffodils on the windowsill and with my aunt's red hair the photo fairly shouts with color and life. In the photo, the window is open and in the distance I can see the cobalt blue of the sea and the powder blue of the sky.

"Oh," I say, my hand reaching for the image of its own accord. It's as though I could touch her. Then my hair fairly lifts off my head when I recognize the rocks in the sea behind her — those are the rocks just off Lavner Bay, the rocks where she drowned. Or was drowned. Or something.

"Powerful, isn't it?" a voice asks from behind me.

I turn and step into the ruins of the raku. "Oh, yeah," I say, embarrassed as hell. The voice belongs to the woman I saw in the coffeeshop, the woman with glasses (Paula Eyde, I presume), and she's holding a dustpan and whisk broom. "I'll pay for the raku," I say. "I'm sorry. The photo . . . it startled me."

"It has that effect on people," she says, tidying up the pieces of pottery. "The others do, too."

I see what she means. Here and there along the same wall with my aunt's photo are life-sized photos of other people, all framed by windows. And all the subjects are, well, older people. Seniors, maybe. Hell, I don't know what the politically correct term is, but they're older people with faces full of character and a life of wisdom in their eyes. I'm blown away.

"These photos . . . I mean they're all so real . . . it's amazing . . ."

"It is, isn't it?" the woman says and I turn back to her. She's somewhere between forty and fifty, with tortoise-shell glasses and lack of makeup that at first glance makes her look plain and severe. But her eyes are a warm brown and she has a kind, open face and a mouth that wants to smile. Here's another woman I could like, I think. "I'm Paula Eyde," she says. "I own the gallery."

"Er, Allie," I reply. "Allie Grace. How much is that one?" I ask, pointing to the painting of my aunt.

"Twelve hundred dollars," she says and I gulp. But I know, I absolutely know that I have to have it. It's expensive, but I can afford it — I just inherited ten grand, after all. "I want to buy it," I hear myself saying and the woman looks at me oddly. "Oh," she says. "Well, that's a very special photograph. You see, the subject just died and I think the photographer wants to give it to, ah, a family member." She turns to look at the photo again. "That's Grace O'Neil. She was a friend of mine. We all loved her a great deal and will miss her terribly. She was so . . . vibrant. Like a flame. She's left an empty place in our lives that nothing can fill up," she says, her voice husky.

Paula loved my aunt, I realize, and unless she's the best actress in the world, there's real pain in her voice.

So here's my chance — I should speak up, claim my birthright for God's sake, but do I? No. I just stand there trying to think of something to say. What does she mean "the photographer wants to give it to a family member" — what family member, pray? I'm the last of the O'Neils. And then it dawns on me. Cordelia. She wants to give it to Cordelia. My aunt's lover. I grind my teeth in frustration. "You said you think the photographer wants to give it to the family," I say. "Does that mean you're not sure or the photographer isn't sure?"

"The photographer isn't sure," she tells me, looking at me oddly. I see her eyes cut from my face to the painting and before I can whip my dark glasses on or turn away, bingo, she's said it. "Why, you look just like Grace," she says in astonishment. "I can see why you might want the photograph. It's really an uncanny resemblance. You're not . . . related, are you?"

"Who, me?" I shake my head vigorously. "No way. Like you said, it's just an uncanny resemblance. One of those fluky things." I look at the photo again and suddenly I have an overwhelming sense of loss. "Could you find out? About the photograph."

Paula is staring at me fixedly and I know, I absolutely know that she doesn't believe that I'm unrelated to Grace. She takes half a step toward me and half-opens her mouth in a wordless *oh*. "Yes," she says, nodding her head, "I'll make a phone call," and hurries to the front of the gallery.

Cripes, now I'm in for it. If I had to bet, I'd bet that the phone call Paula's going to make isn't about the picture at all — it's about me. And if I'm right, that tells me several things — that Cordelia shared the contents of my aunt's will with her friends, and that they're on the lookout for me. Recalling my not-too-bright attempt at an alias when I checked into the B & B, I cringe. Cordelia's probably known who I am since she ran my Visa card.

Paula returns from the front of the gallery, looking flustered. "The photographer still isn't sure what she wants to do," she informs me, adjusting her glasses, avoiding my eyes. "But it's my feeling that she'll probably give the picture to Grace's relative."

"Rats," I say, testing the waters. "Is the family member a local? I mean, maybe I could buy it from him. Or her."

"Maybe you could," she tells me, giving me a look that's full of anxiety and yes, there it is again — guilt. Another of the Sisters Who Know Something. "Why don't you leave me your name and phone number."

"Sure," I say, determined to play out this charade to the end. Paula doesn't seem as fragile as Robin and besides, she doesn't have a cat, so how nice can she *really* be? I scribble my name, well, my alias, and my California address and phone number on a scrap of paper and hand it to Paula. While I'm at it, I write her a check for the broken raku. "I'll be at the Lavner Bay Bed and Breakfast for a few more days," I tell her, in case she doesn't know. She takes the piece of paper and looks up at me in alarm and I realize that no, she didn't know. And suddenly I can't think of anything else to say. Short of casting aside my alias and revealing myself to the world as the Avenging Heiress. And I'm not quite ready to do that. Not yet.

Chapter 9

So I blew it, I guess. I got absolutely no information out of either Robin or Paula. Only a feeling that Robin's a really decent human being who couldn't possibly have had anything to do with Aunt Grace's death. And Paula — well, Paula's a business-woman and a little colder, but my take on her is that she loved my aunt and couldn't have had anything to do with her death either. But what's in a feeling? So Robin has a cat and a pretty house and makes a living out of helping people — so what? She could still be an ax murderer, couldn't she? And

Paula said that she loved my aunt. Big deal. People in the books I sell sometimes seem to be equally loving, caring people — and then turn out to be guilty of the most atrocious crimes. Nor do you have to turn to fiction to find such folk, I remind myself. Just turn on the six o'clock news. ("Gosh, she was such a *nice* lady! Wouldn't hurt a fly.") But when I think myself back inside Robin's kitchen, holding the purring Amberilla, or hear again the pain in Paula's voice, I get that feeling again.

Okay, okay, I tell myself, but what about that other stuff — Robin's alarm when I mentioned the subject of my so-called relative's possible murder and Paula's anxious guilt after she made her phone call? What do those responses mean? Quite possibly that neither lady is directly involved (I don't want anyone with a cat as terrific as Amberilla to be directly involved) but that both of them may well have, as they say in the trade, guilty knowledge. The same guilty knowledge that Bree and Ossie have. But how do I find out what that knowledge is?

What the hell am I supposed to do now? I suppose an experienced investigator (Kerry, maybe) would know how to proceed — march back and trick, wheedle, or bully the truth out of the recalcitrant Robin and the prim Paula. I, however, am at a loss. I lean against the hood of the Escort, chew a hangnail, and think about my nonexistent people skills. Hey, I haven't chosen to make my living doing mail-order books for no reason. There's an immense sense of freedom and relief in not having to ever deal with living, breathing people.

I'm getting pretty grumpy — I always get that way when I need to eat — and because I can't think of a better place to go, I head back to the crabbing dock near Coast Seafoods, intending to get a sandwich or something. I park the Escort and lean against the hood for a few minutes, enjoying the nice, cool afternoon air, watching the tourists come and go with their crab rings. What do they do with the crabs they catch, I wonder, spying a couple in celery-colored polo shirts and white shorts, burdened with a ring, heading over to the rental hut. Maybe I'm about to find out. A kid behind the counter takes the ring and empties out a crab — a big one, waving its claws in indignation. He checks the crab (I think I read somewhere that females have to be thrown back), disappears into the hut, and reappears out back where he lifts the lid on a steaming barrel and unceremoniously tosses the poor crab in.

And that's when it hits me if. If you multiply the scene on this little dock by a thousand or so, how can there possibly be enough crabs to go around? Or other fish, for that matter? I mean, sure, the coast doesn't have billboards, but as soon as you hit any burg of more than two people and a dog you get signs proclaiming "Albacore and Fries," "Smoked Salmon," "Fresh Oysters," until you begin to wonder if there can be anything left swimming in the sea. Actually, that's not so far-fetched a proposition. Yesterday, I read in the local rag that wild salmon are disappearing from Oregon rivers and that pretty soon the salmon industry will have to depend on hatchery-grown salmon. Between clear-cutting (which encourages hillside erosion, choking up the rivers) and overfishing, there just aren't many wild salmon left. Except on Indian lands. I remember now that Native Americans are called Indians here — by themselves and others — so I guess it's the politically correct thing to do. I'll have to tell Kerry.

The celery-shirted couple have walked around to the back of the crab hut where they wait by the barrel, laughing and talking, and even though it's a male crab being boiled alive in there, I feel a little sick. I mean, couldn't the kid have whacked it with a brick or something before dropping it in hot water? Does torture improve flavor? Maybe it's my low blood sugar or incipient depression but I have this sudden vision of jillions of crabs being dropped alive into jillions of barrels up and down the coast, and thousands of albacore and salmon and who-knows-what flopping and gasping on the decks of fishing boats, sending their silent screams off into the cosmos. I'm horrified — at my vision and at what's happening to me. I mean, until just this moment, I hadn't spent more than two seconds thinking about crabs, but suddenly they seem pretty darned important. To me they don't seem much different from the whale we all oohed and aahed over at Drizzle Bay and I suddenly know that I could never eat another crab. Ever. This epiphany is so intense that I clutch the hood of the Escort for support, feeling like I've had a vision. Well, maybe I have.

I'm awed, ashamed, and depressed all at once and I feel like running across the parking lot and asking Robin if she can help me. *I'm suffering from cosmic grief. I just heard the death cries of a million fish.* Then I'm laughing and crying together and after I recover from *that,* an intense desire to get the hell out of here washes over me. Would Aunt Grace understand if I just bailed out? What's left of my mind snaps me back to the attorney's office a couple days ago when I declared with admirable firmness that I didn't want the B & B. So why am I still here? True, Aunt Grace saved my life when I was a kid, but isn't this sudden debt I feel toward her ninety percent guilt? I mean, she dutifully wrote me a nice card every Christmas and every birthday and what did I send her back? Nada. At the time, I didn't feel *too* guilty for not responding because I really, truly did intend to write to her, it's just that I . . . didn't get around to it. And now there's no time. Her death put an end to that possibility. Death is so damned final, isn't it — suddenly there's no time to make amends, to set things straight, to start again.

And what about Grace? Would she have wanted me to pry the lid off her life and poke around in it? Because that's what I'm going to have to do if I continue with this so-called investigation. After my talk with Dee and her revelation about Grace's being gay, I've realized that not only my aunt's death but her life as well will come under Kerry's and my scrutiny. And it just doesn't seem . . . right.

I wipe my eyes on the tail of my T-shirt, sniffle a little, and fish in my pocket for the piece of paper on which I've written the names of Delia's cronies. *There's nothing you can do about a million fish deaths, but there is something you can do about Aunt Grace's. Just find out what really happened. Either she learned to swim or she didn't. Either she drowned or she didn't. Keep it simple, stupid.* I often have to talk to myself like this — remind myself what I'm supposed to be doing and why I'm doing it. Comes from living alone, I guess.

So who's next? Mary White? Whitney No-Last-Name? There's a phone booth beside the crab hut and I walk over, thumbing listlessly through the pages, not expecting any help. But to my surprise, there she is. Mary White, it seems, is an insurance agent right here in Windsock.

And then, of course, there's Delia. It's oh, so tempting to make an end-run around all these inquiries and just come right out and buttonhole her. And then what? If she's as involved as I think she is (and I'm beginning to think of her as a spider lurking in the center of a very sticky web) she wouldn't tell me zip. Instead, she'd be on the phone pronto to the Sisters Who Know Something and they'd all clam up or take vacations and then where would I be?

I squint into the sun, looking across the bay at the green hill on the river's opposite shore. Sooner or later, I realize, I may well have to involve the police and the very thought makes my palms sweat. All those large men with creaking gun belts and body odor. I'm sure they would take me seriously — I look so much like a regular, respectable citizen.

All this thinking has put quite an edge on my appetite and as if I conjured it up, a delicious odor wafts over to me and I sniff, following it like a hound on a trail. A family of six wanders out of Coast Seafoods bearing goodies in little bags — take-out french fries! My stomach gurgles in approval and I sigh. Do I dare? What the hell. They probably won't remember me.

Bad luck. The young guy with the buzz cut at the cash register at Coast gives me a look of recognition as soon as I walk in.

"You can sit over there while you wait," he says, writing up my order and indicating a couple of chairs in a corner by the door. I sit, picking up a newspaper to hide behind, hoping no multiples of two will come in and give me pitying looks while they wait for a table. Or worse yet, talk to me. No one really knows what to make of single people in restaurants, do they? A waitress once asked me if I minded sharing my table with someone and then she got *extremely* huffy when I said yes, I did. So I've given up eating out. The Chinese and Mexican places around the corner from my place prepare great takeout meals and Sammy is always an attentive dining companion. Come to think of it, the seafood dinner I had with Kerry was the first meal I'd had in a fancy restaurant in years. Not since . . . not since the fiftieth birthday dinner with Aunt Grace and my mother the year Mom died. Well, that's definitely something I don't want to think about.

"Your order will be up in a couple of minutes," the kid says.

"Thanks," I tell him, pathetically grateful that he wasn't actively unpleasant. Because after the crying jag brought on by the thought of crab deaths, and musings on my mother and Aunt Grace, I'm not feeling my usual on-top-of-things self. If I had to tell the truth — and I often avoid doing so, particularly to myself — I'd have to admit that I'm afraid of people who are unpleasant, especially men. They have big rough hands and loud voices and calculating eyes and (maybe I'm imagining things here) I sense in them a barely controlled propensity for violence that makes me want to run. Don't get me wrong, though — if I have to stand up for myself, I can yell and scream

108

with the best of them, but for the most part I try to avoid confrontations.

Lately, though, I've been thinking that I need to get out more, go places, do things, but exactly how to do it and with whom in Lancaster has me kind of stumped. I haven't had a whole lot of practice being social. Bradley and I go out to a movie now and then, but it doesn't count because we're not really *together*, if you know what I mean. And it's pretty depressing because wherever we go there are these Noah's ark couples, male and female side by side, one of each. Bradley wants to take me to LA to some gay bars, but I'm not much of a drinker and to tell the truth I'm absolutely, completely petrified that I might meet someone like Melanie, you know, someone that I'd fall head over heels in love with and follow to some even more godforsaken place than Lancaster. So even though Bradley says I'm perverse, I've nixed the gay bar proposition. That doesn't mean I don't want to meet someone because I do, but I just want it to be . . . different. Slower. Sweeter.

I'm sitting here thinking about singles and couples and such things when a female voice says, "Hey, you, I wanna talk to you a minute." I look up and it's the older Indian woman, the one I talked to yesterday, the one who glared and muttered. She's definitely low on the list of people I want to talk to, but I seem to have no choice in the matter.

"Sure," I say magnanimously.

"It's about Kerry," she begins and I nod. I mean, who else do we have in common — Mother Teresa? "You're a friend of hers, right?"

I consider this. "Not exactly. We're working together."

"Same thing," she says and I begin to get a little irritated. "I'm gonna tell you something and I want you to tell Kerry. Okay?"

"Well now, I'm not too comfortable with that," I say. "Couldn't you tell her yourself? After all, her office is upstairs."

"Useta be upstairs," the woman says. "Tell her I want her to go. Here's her stuff." She waddles around the cash register and produces a green garbage bag, secured with a tie tag. "I know she's running," the crone says, "but she can't run from the bad luck. You tell her that."

"Excuse me? The bad luck?"

"A man," she says. "A man was here this morning. He asked for her. He had eyes that wanted to eat someone up."

I'm actively alarmed now. "What man? Did he say who he was? What he wanted?"

"The bad luck is using him to find Kerry," she says, plunging ahead with her monologue. "Tell her to stay away from here. To stay away from us." She prods the bag with one foot. "Take her stuff," she commands. If I had fur, it would be bristling by now and I'd be baring my teeth in a snarl.

"We shouldn't turn our backs on her, Ma," the young man says. "If she's in trouble —"

Ma says something to him dismissively in another language, adding for, my benefit, in English, "When my sister took the *na-set* I heard it cry. I hear it cry still. It is very bad luck to take a *na-set* but the bad luck must stay with my sister's child. I do not want it to come to us. I do not want it visiting this family.

Tell her," she pokes my arm for emphasis, "to stay away. She is not family. I have cast her out."

"Ma —" the kid says again, but the old woman cuts him off.

"You shut up, you," she tells him, and I'm about to get up and leave, fries or no fries, when the crone clamps a hand on my arm. "We know what happened to Kerry in Portland. The bad luck found her there. We don't want her bringing her trouble here."

"Oh, Ma, for Christ's sake," the kid says. "There's no such thing as bad luck." Someone from the kitchen appears at precisely that moment and hands him a bag. I pry the old lady's fingers off my arm and stand, hoping the bag from the kitchen has my order in it. "Don't pay any attention to her," he tells me, and at this, Ma reaches over and whacks him with a menu, disappearing into the back of the restaurant. "She's just superstitious," he says, handing me my order. Reluctantly, he drags the green garbage bag toward me. "You better take it or Ma will throw it out. She means what she said. Tell Kerry that Daniel says hi. And if she needs help . . ."

"Yeah, sure, I'll tell her," I reassure him, wanting only to flee this place.

What a family! I take my fries and the garbage bag back to the car, wondering how Kerry stood living with the reproachful matriarch for as long as she did. But then, I guess if you've been burned out of car and home, you might have to come back to your family. Even if the Wicked Witch of the West kept muttering "bad luck" every time she saw you? What a fate. Well, Kerry was well rid of them.

Still, a tiny little piece of what Ma had said in there made sense — the bit about Kerry's trouble following her to the coast. I had no idea what the aunt was talking about when she raved on about the stolen *na-set* and I certainly didn't believe in bad luck, but I did believe in the tenacity of hit men (hey, mysteries are full of tales of such terriers). There was no point in jumping to conclusions, but maybe I ought to let Kerry know about the man whose eyes wanted to eat something up. (I decide not to tell her how vehement Ma was that she keep her bad luck to herself — no one needs to know something like that.) But the more I think about the mystery caller, the antsier I get. After all, I don't want my investigator wearing cement overshoes, now do I? I toss the garbage bag in the back of my car, scarf down my fries, and decide I'd better go see about Kerry.

Chapter 10

I don't know what I expected, but inside the
out-of-business motel's main house, Kerry's as happy
as a clam, sitting at her one table behind a barricade
of business machines. I'm relieved to see she's
obviously okay, busily clacking away on the keyboard
of her new computer while about fifty yards of faxes
lie on the floor in front of her.

"Hi," she says, looking up as I come in. The
phone rings again, the fax beeps, and another few
feet of paper are disgorged from its innards. "Hmmm,

we're going to need another paper roll if this keeps up."

I pick up one end of the fax. "What's this? The condensed version of *War and Peace*?"

"Funny," she says. "No, it's a bunch of reports. Police, forensics — like that. I'm expecting credit and financial information next." She peers at the material spewing out of the fax. "Oh, good," she says happily. "So, what've you been up to?"

"Nothing as productive as that," I tell her, flopping down on the floor beside the fax paper. "So, can I take a look?"

She picks up a pair of scissors and, limping heavily, comes around to join me on the floor. "Let me cut it apart and make some folders and then we can look at it together." She takes the paper back to her table where I hear her snipping away.

"You love this stuff, don't you?"

"Sorry, what?"

"Sleuthing by computer. Accumulating piles of stuff. Arranging it."

"Uh huh. And I'm good at it, too. Okay, let's take a look. Police report first."

I hoist myself up and go around the table to join her and am immediately struck by how many teeny tiny little compartments the report has and how lousy the handwriting is. My old Document Block resurfaces and I start to panic. I'm never going to be able to read this. "I can't . . . can you tell me what it says?" I ask Kerry.

She looks at me strangely, then shrugs. "Sure. The police were called at approximately eight p.m. the evening of August eleventh by Cordelia Norville. She reported that Grace O'Neil had gone snorkeling about four o'clock as was her habit and had failed to return. Her boat was still anchored at the rocks offshore, Miss Norville said."

"Eight o'clock? Why did she wait so long to call the cops? I thought they missed Grace at dinner?"

Kerry scribbles the question down on a yellow legal tablet. "Dunno. We'll ask. Let's go on.

"Officer . . . Renquist responded to the call and visited the B & B about nine that evening. Blah, blah, blah, took a report, went down to the beach, looked out to sea at the rocks where Miss O'Neil usually anchored to snorkel, saw that the Whaler was still there, and called the Coast Guard."

"Oh yeah? No one told me that." But then, no one had really told me anything. I swallow, as if this were a story whose plot I'm following closely, hoping the heroine will be found alive. Only it's not a story, and I already know the ending. This heroine was found dead.

Kerry rummaged around in the pile of unfiled faxes. "So there ought to be a Coast Guard report here, too. Not here, not here . . . okay, I guess I'd better get on the phone and ask for it . . . no, here it is."

"Jeez," I say admiringly. "How did you get all this stuff?"

She grins wolfishly. "Your power of attorney, my businesslike demeanor, the invocation of Pinkerton's name, and a dash of insistence."

I'm really, truly impressed. Compared to my seat-of-the-pants efforts, Kerry's approach is positively . . . professional.

"Okay, let's take a look at what the Coast Guard had to say. A cutter was dispatched from the

Nautilus station, arrived at the rocks off Lavner Bay just after eleven, located the Whaler belonging to the B & B, searched the rocks and found the body of an adult female. They returned the Whaler to the B & B's dock and took the body back to their Nautilus station after calling the sheriff to meet them there. The report ends there."

"What? They took the body? Did they get any photos of, you know, the crime scene?"

Kerry's silent, thumbing through the pages. "Nope. Maybe the police report says something about photos." More ruffling of pages. "Nope again. No photos. The sheriff called the county morgue from the Coast Guard station and the medical examiner's personnel came to get the body at about two a.m."

Kerry flipped through the pages. "Here's Cordelia Neville's statement if you want to read it."

"You bet I do," I say, fairly snatching it from her.

"I'll look for the medical examiner's report," Kerry tells me gently.

I walk over to the window where there's better light and smooth out the crinkled pages of Cordelia's statement. It isn't long and as I skim it, I realize that the high points are in the police report — that Grace had taken the Whaler and gone snorkeling at four as she did every day; that the Lavner Bay ladies missed Grace at supper and started looking for her; that Delia called the police about eight. End of story.

"Did the police talk to anyone besides Cordelia?" I ask Kerry.

"Let me see." She rustles around in her papers. "They talked to Pan — she and Cordelia both looked for Grace when she didn't show up for supper. That seems to be it."

"Ha!" I yell. "Didn't anyone think this so-called snorkeling was awfully strange behavior for a fifty-year-old woman?"

Kerry shrugs. "Why should they? Lots of fifty-year-olds are fit enough to snorkel in the ocean."

I give her a dirty look. "No one takes a boat out alone. That's elementary water safety."

Another shrug. "She thought she was safe. After all, it's less than a quarter-mile from shore."

"What's the official cause of death, anyhow? Did you find the medical examiner's report yet?"

"Yeah, I just found it," Kerry says. "Let's take a look."

I go back to join her at the fax machine and again the compartments filled with scrubbling defeat me. "Tell me," I ask her grimly.

"Um, okay. Because all unattended deaths are treated as suspicious circumstances, a very careful examination of the body was made."

"Careful? How careful? Did they do an autopsy?"

"No autopsy."

"Were any blood samples drawn? Did anyone check for, you know, drugs or alcohol?"

Kerry shakes her head. "Doesn't look like it. Well, at least someone really did *examine* the body — here are the M.E.'s notes. There were several deep cuts on the hands noted here but it's thought these were consistent with the victim's trying to pull herself out of the sea and up onto the rocks. Apart from that — nothing significant. No blows to the head, no

117

bruising. Water in the lungs indicates that the victim did indeed drown, and core temperature indicates that she drowned sometime that evening." Kerry looks up from the report. "The cause of death is listed as hypothermia leading to drowning."

I shake my head. "No way. Kerry, this is a woman who couldn't even *swim*. Who was afraid of the water."

"I guess she got over it. Cordelia's sworn statement says she snorkeled. Every day."

I glower at her.

"Okay," Kerry says brightly. "Here's what we need to do. We need to find someone who saw Grace go out in the Whaler. Cordelia said she went out every day about four, didn't she?"

"Yeah," I say cautiously.

"So we need to talk to someone who saw her. And because you suspect them of something, we ought not to rely on the recollections of the other people at Lavner Bay." She closes one of the file folders and squares up the pile she's assembled. Then she looks at me a little oddly. "Allison, if you don't mind my asking, what exactly is it that you suspect?"

"What do I suspect?" I'm flabbergasted. "What do you mean?"

"I mean that here we have an M.E.'s report that basically found nothing suspicious. As hard as this is for you to accept, maybe this was a perfectly straightforward drowning."

I'm stunned. "I can't believe I'm hearing this from you. Earlier, when I explained things to you, you said the case looked interesting, that it had merits."

"Yes, but that was before I saw the reports," she says reasonably. God, I hate reasonable people.

"And now?"

"Now, I'd have to agree with them. That your aunt just ... drowned."

I count to ten so I don't start yelling. "Okay. Maybe she did." I see Kerry frowning at me and amend my statement. "Okay, I agree too. She drowned. I can accept that. What I can't accept is that she well, snorkeled."

"So we're back at the eyewitness," Kerry says. "Right?"

"Right."

"So we need to find one. Then we can rule the snorkeling in or out."

"What's your gut feeling about this?" I ask her. "I can't think straight anymore."

"I usually don't put much faith in gut instincts," she says, "but my feeling after reading the reports is that if we can get independent corroboration of the fact that Grace snorkeled, then we ought to be satisfied. I know I'll be satisfied."

I exhale slowly, trying to be reasonable like Kerry. Hell, maybe she's right. "Okay, the eyewitness. What do we do?"

"Is there a house close by? Another inn? A motel? A business — anything that would have a direct view of the bay and those rocks?"

I close my eyes and try to remember. "I think so. There's a bunch of cabins on the northwest side of the bay." I fish in my pants pocket for my car keys. "Well?" I say. "Let's go."

Kerry shakes her head. "What — right now? I'm

119

waiting for some more documents. Besides," she grimaces, "I don't pound the pavement. Remember?"

"Yeah," I say testily, "I remember. So I'll do it."

"You will?"

Duh — who else? "Yeah. I'll do it. It's just — asking questions. Trying to find someone who saw something. Anything."

"I don't think you ought to," Kerry says. "If you get names and telephone numbers, I can —"

"Oh hell, I've been doing it all day," I tell her, confessing to my impromptu gumshoe activities with Robin and Paula.

"Amazing," she says. "I don't know if I would have had the nerve to do things quite that way."

"Yeah, well, it's because you're left-brained and I'm right-brained, I guess." Or hare-brained. "So, I might as well carry on asking questions." Because, yes, she did tell me she didn't pound the pavement and even if she was willing to do so, I figure she'd really appreciate not having to walk all over Oregon tomorrow on her bum leg.

I can see the idea appeals to her. "Well . . . okay."

"Sure," I say, fairly itching to get out of there.

"Be careful though," she tells me. "Don't spook anyone."

I'm already halfway out the door. "No problem."

"Wait," she calls and I turn around.

She's taking something out of a folder and holding it up to me. I go back for it, and as she hands it to me I realize what it must be. "It's a photo of your aunt," Kerry says, confirming my guess. I cringe a little as I take it, expecting it to be a faxed photo of her body, but no, it's a photo of her sitting on the deck of the B & B. She's (was) a handsome, long-haired woman and she's laughing, both arms spread out as if to embrace something vast. It's like a punch in the heart because she looks just the way I remember her from our dinner five years ago. And she looks so . . . alive. Just the way she looked in the photo in Paula's gallery. Guilt threatens to settle down on me like a cloud and I mutter, "Thanks," and hurry out of the office before I'm smothered.

So I'm feeling a tiny bit depressed and a bigger bit preoccupied as I get into the Escort and roll out onto 101. I'm halfway down the hill before I realize: I forgot to tell Kerry what I came for. About the man whose eyes want to eat something up. And the garbage bag full of stuff. But cars are honking at me so I pick up the pace. I'll just have to tell her later, I mutter to myself. She'll be all right. After all, there's no way the man with the eyes can find her at her new place.

Chapter 11

Twelve smallish brown cabins nestled in a woodsy
five acres just south of the B & B proclaim themselves
to be the Cloverleaf Cabins — a name which is
downright silly, if you ask me, considering that
there's nary a cloverleaf in sight. Nevertheless, the
three waterfront cabins have a dynamite view of
Lavner Bay and maybe, just maybe, one of the guests
saw something. I park on the little drive behind the
cabins and get out, walking down to the beach to get
a different view of the rocks where Aunt Grace
supposedly died. I'm directly across Lavner Bay from

the B & B so the view I'm getting of the rocks includes the spot where Aunt Grace supposedly anchored the Whaler when she went on her famous snorkeling expeditions. I walk along the drive, the beach on my right, the cabins on my left until the motel's property ends. I've never been along this drive so I'm surprised to see a number of private homes strung out along the little road. I'm encouraged by this. Maybe these folks — and there do seem to be a few of them out in the yards gardening, washing cars, and just hanging out on their decks — would be a more likely source of information. After all, they're a presumably permanent population. Still, someone in the cabins might have seen something, so I decide to start there first.

As luck would have it, I've hit the cabins in that twilight zone time between check-out and check-in when all the room cleaners are scurrying around trying to get things shipshape and there's nary a guest in sight. Still, I have to ask. The door to Number Four is open so I go inside. A greasy-haired blonde kid of no more than 16 in cut-off jeans and an oversized flannel shirt is carrying a load of wadded-up bedding out to her cart which is stationed on the little flagstone walk outside. Seeing me, she removes a pair of headphones and parks her gum someplace in her mouth which will allow for free speech.

"Check-in time isn't until four," she tells me, looking me curiously up and down.

"I don't want a room. There was a drowning in the bay about a week ago," I say authoritatively. "Were you working that day?"

"Oh yeah," she says, her interest clearly piqued.

"I remember that. Some old lady fell out of her boat or something and drowned."

"Were you working?" I repeat, telling myself not to get aggravated.

"Nah. My day off."

"Who was working that day?" I ask with uncharacteristic patience. She wrinkles her brow, concentrating as though this was the final question on *Wheel of Fortune. The category is Person. Person. You have ten seconds to answer the puzzle in the category Person. Begin.* Finally the answer comes to her. "It was Elsie," she says.

"And Elsie is . . ." I let the question hang.

"Oh, she's off today," the kid says, giving her gum a few vigorous chomps.

No kidding. "When will she be back on?" I inquire.

"What do you want to know about the drowning for?" the kid asks curiously. "Are you a reporter or something?"

She's given me an open field, an invitation to lie, and I have to admit, the offer is tempting. I do so much better with people when I'm pretending to be someone else (I'm not in the fantasy business for nothing, right?) but I just can't seem to summon up the energy right now. Still, a reporter . . . yeah, I could be a reporter. Instead, I hear myself say, "I'm the dead woman's niece," and I'm so shocked I have to pause for a moment. In one instant, I've shed my protective coat of prevarication and for one terrified instant I feel naked and vulnerable, like something cowering under a bush. And then suddenly, unaccountably, I feel . . . powerful. Terrific. I feel like . . . like an avenging angel. All I need is a fiery sword.

Hot damn — is this what the truth does for you? Maybe I should try it more often. "I want to know what happened," I tell the kid.

She shrugs. "I dunno. She drowned. That's what the newspaper said."

I groan. This kid is definitely not even *Wheel of Fortune* material. My cat Sam could do better than this — and Sam's a devoted *Wheel* watcher. I haven't figured out if it's the movement of the wheel or Vanna White he's attracted to. "So when will Elsie be back?"

"Tomorrow," the kid says doubtfully, then with growing certainty, "yeah, tomorrow. For sure."

"Thanks," I tell her. "I'll come back then."

So, that seems to take care of the cabins. I'm feeling let down, but I tell myself not to be discouraged, that surely someone along here saw something. Thus fortified, I approach the first home. I knock and ring, but no one comes to the door. Strike one. At the second house, an old gent in the driveway is just finishing washing his car. When he sees me coming up the driveway, he takes his bucket, retreats into his garage, and before I can say "Hi!" the garage door descends with a definitive clatter. Strike two. At the third house, an elderly woman in a denim work shirt, khaki pants, and a blue floppy hat is digging in her flower bed. I approach tentatively, trying my best to look nonthreatening. What do I have to do — roll over and present my underbelly?

"Hi," I say.

She looks up in surprise. "Well, hello," she says looking me over with frank interest. I try not to feel irked — at least she's not running for her garage.

"Lovely view you have," I tell her.

"Yes, it is, isn't it. We bought the house for the view." She leans on her shovel and when I don't amble on down the road, she senses that I want something. "Can I, ah, help you?"

"Maybe," I confess, coming a little closer, hoping I'm not invading her personal space. "There was a drowning in the bay last week. The lady who died, well, she was my aunt." Oops. There it was again. The truth. Well, it's out now. Who knows — maybe it will prove to be more useful than a lie.

"Oh, I'm sorry for you," she says with enough warmth to make it the truth.

I'm encouraged and step a little closer. "Thanks. Well, anyway, I'm trying to find someone who might have seen the boat she was on anchor at those rocks out there."

She looks at me, one eyebrow raised.

"I thought you might have seen it because you live right here."

"Are you really a relative?"

"Yes ma'am." I dig in my pocket for my wallet, flipping it open to my California driver's license. "See — Allison O'Neil. Same last name as the woman who drowned. Grace O'Neil. My aunt."

She looks my license over carefully, finally handing it back to me. "So you're Grace's niece. And you've come for our information. Very well."

"Your information — you did see something, didn't you?"

"Yes and no. It may be nothing, but we — Jane and I — always thought it odd that no one from the police came around to ask us any questions. Not that I particularly want to answer people's questions, you understand, but still, I did think it odd, with a drowning and all."

I shrug. "I guess they felt the circumstances weren't suspicious."

She raises her eyebrow again, and I edge even closer.

"I'm surprised, too," I say. Then, "What did you mean by 'yes and no'?"

"Well, the newspaper accounts of the story reported that it was Grace's habit to take the Whaler out to the rocks over there every day."

"You mean she didn't go every day?"

"No, not every day. And when the boat did go out, Cordelia and Grace were in it together. I don't recall seeing Grace ever take the boat out by herself as the newspaper account reported. Moreover," she says, wrinkling her brow a little, "the story made it sound as though this boating and snorkeling was a lifelong habit of Grace's, when in reality it was fairly new."

"New? How new?"

"I've only noticed the Whaler out there at the rocks since, oh, the Fourth of July."

"Are you sure?" I ask, excited.

She gives me a sharp look. "Of course I'm sure. I may be old, but I'm not addle-brained. Not yet. The afternoon of the Fourth of July was the first time I laid eyes on that boat. I remember because there was a fireworks display in town — we saw it from here — but before that the Whaler motored out to the rocks and had its own fireworks party."

"Really — a party? Who was there? Could you see?"

"Some of them, yes. It was just after supper —

there was still plenty of light. I was able to recognize your aunt by her red hair and Cordelia by her silver hair. I happened to be out here because I was setting up our lawn chairs on the deck to watch the fireworks. As for the other people in the boat, I can't tell you if they were young or old, male or female, but I counted four others."

Four people: the cast of characters from the B & B or the ladies from the espresso bar? I feel that I'm maybe onto something here, but I wonder just how reliable this old gal is.

She must be reading my thoughts, because she says, "I've been out here every day rain or shine since the first of June, digging the ivy out of these flower beds. I sit right there on that log and have a cup of tea about four o'clock. I assure you — I would have seen the Whaler if it had been there earlier. But it wasn't."

"So after the fireworks party in July, the Whaler went out to the rocks, what, two or three times a week?"

She nods. "Sometimes. Sometimes every other day."

I'm trying to make sense of this so I repeat what she said to me earlier. "And Cordelia was always with my aunt."

"Yes. As I said, she was easy to recognize because of her silver hair."

"And my aunt by her red hair," I repeat. "So, did you see the Whaler the day of the ... the day my aunt drowned?"

She nods, looking anxious. "Yes."

"Did you notice anything unusual?"

She shakes her head firmly. "No. Nothing. I've

128

reviewed that day in my mind — just in case anyone came to ask for information — but everything seemed the same as every other day."

"But —" I clam up to think about this. If Cordelia went out with my aunt that day, then how could she have been the one at the B & B who wondered why Grace hadn't come back and started a search? I'm genuinely alarmed now. There seems to be a considerable discrepancy between what this woman saw and what Delia told the cops and the newspaper.

"Tea should be along, oh, right about now." I look at my watch. Five to four.

As if on cue, the front door of the house opens and another spry-looking old lady, this one in green polyester pants and a yellow polo shirt, comes out to join us, two steaming mugs in her hand. "Teatime," she says brightly, handing the flower-bed-digger one of the mugs. "Lemon Mist today," she says, looking me up and down curiously. "I'm Jane. And she's Margaret. I don't imagine she introduced herself — too much communing with Nature makes one forget one's manners. Young lady, would you like a cup of tea?"

"Oh, well, um, I don't think so," I say. "But thanks anyhow." My brain is buzzing with what Margaret just told me and frankly I don't give a rat's ass about manners or tea or anything else right now.

Margaret turns to Jane, indignant. "I have most definitely not forgotten my manners. This young lady is Allison O'Neil," she says. "Grace's niece."

Jane looks at me with shrewd blue eyes. "So, someone did come after all. We wondered if anyone would."

"Didn't you think this information was important enough to go to someone with? The police, maybe?" I ask. "Because I sure as heck think it's important."

They look at each other. "We weren't sure. We did try to get in touch with that newspaper reporter so she could correct things, but the police?" Jane sips her tea thoughtfully. "Allison, we're a couple of old women and old women traditionally don't have all their marbles. Besides, we weren't completely sure that our information meant anything at all."

"Apart from the fact that the reporter had gotten things wrong," Margaret adds. "Accuracy in journalism is a particular peeve of mine."

"You're sometimes a little too concerned with accuracy," Jane says critically to Margaret. "It can get tedious." She turns to me. "She used to teach it, you see. Journalism, that is. Not accuracy."

"Oh for heaven's sake, they're one and the same," Margaret says testily and I'm a little put off by their public airing of what is plainly a private, ongoing disagreement.

"And we might as well be honest — this isn't the first thing Margaret's called to correct reporter Kristin about." Jane looks at me. "Margaret's a stickler for good writing as well as good reporting. It's understandable that Kristin might not have been eager to return the phone call."

"You see our dilemma," Margaret says. "We had a piece of information and didn't quite know what to do with it. So we just decided to wait. We figured if anyone really needed to know, they'd come around asking questions."

They sip their tea and look at me. "So now you

have the information. Does it help you with your quest?" Margaret asks.

"My . . . quest? I wasn't aware I was on one." I'm shocked that this old lady can so easily see right through me.

"Of course you are," Margaret says. "You have that look about you. Grim. Determined."

"For heaven's sake, don't be so melodramatic," Jane says.

"I'm not," Margaret objects. "It's there to see if you only look."

"You wanted to know if the information helps?" I repeat, to break up this latest skirmish. "I guess I'd have to say yes and no. It's answered a big question I had, but it raises another one too. You see, I wasn't aware that my aunt snorkeled, or even swam. She saved my life when I was four by wading in and pulling me out of an undertow when we were at the beach. She was a nonswimmer before that — she had a real fear of the water — and that episode was so traumatic that I just couldn't see her taking up water sports in her fifties. Although," I admit, "we were out of touch for about five years." I'm silent, thinking. "But you've confirmed a couple of things for me. That my aunt really did go out on the Whaler. And that she really did snorkel. God, that's amazing — I can hardly picture it." I'm silent again, trying to see my aunt paddling around calmly in water she heretofore feared. Oh well. Everything changes, I guess.

"You said the information raised a question in your mind?" Margaret asks.

It sure does — the question of why Delia would

131

have lied about being on the boat. It's beginning to look as though this juicy piece of information wasn't an oversight or a reporter's error, but deliberate misdirection on Delia's part. But why? I decide not to alarm Margaret with it. "Oh, nothing important."

The two of them are quiet for a moment, sipping their tea. They apparently have nothing else to tell me, so I get up to go. "Thanks," I say. "Oh, if I have any other questions, would you mind if I phone you?"

"Not at all," Jane says graciously. "We're in the book. Barclay." Yikes — another couple of sisters? Like the Emilys? Or are they real sisters? Or are they Bree's kind of sisters? Oh hell, who cares.

"There is one point I'd like to clear up," Margaret says as they walk me to the road. "Simply because I'm such a stickler for accuracy."

I'm preoccupied now — the revelation that my aunt really had taken up snorkeling has pretty much taken the wind out of my sails. But Margaret's information has raised other suspicions in my mind, along with a theory that isn't fully formed yet but whose details are becoming clearer to me. "Uh huh," I say, more out of politeness than interest.

Margaret hesitates, and Jane bursts out, "Not that silly thing you told me — don't be ridiculous! Really, Meg, you can carry accuracy too far! Let Allison go now."

Suddenly I'm tired of their squabbling — they're just like any married couple who have lived with each other's eccentricities for too long. I wait for Margaret to say something but she defers to Jane and gives me a shrug and a smile.

"I'm staying at the B & B if you think of

anything else," I say. But I really don't think I'll hear from them again. I mean, what else could Margaret have to tell me? The color of Cordelia's windbreaker? God knows, she's told me everything else she noticed. "Thanks for your help," I call over my shoulder as I make my way back to the car. Behind me, I hear them erupt in a fresh round of nattering and I walk a little faster. Silly old things.

Chapter 12

I'm sitting in my car, trying to think, but a talkative raven perched on a picnic table is disturbing my thought processes with nonstop raucous comments. I guess he wants me to feed him, so I rummage around on the floor, find a greasy french fry, and toss it at him. He springs into the air, catches the morsel on the wing, and flies off for parts unknown to savor his treasure, leaving me in peace. So everyone was right and I was wrong — my aunt really was a snorkeler. Okay, okay, I buy it. That point had loomed so large in my mind that I couldn't get past it, and now that it's been confirmed, it hardly matters. Because there's a huge, mountainous discrepancy between what Cordelia told the police and what Margaret swears she saw — that Grace really didn't go out alone and that the Whaler didn't go out every day. The latter point probably doesn't mean anything, but the former? I drum my fingers on the steering wheel, thinking. It means that Cordelia was on the boat with my aunt the afternoon she died. Jesus. I clutch the steering wheel and lean my head against my hands as a host of other things come bubbling up to the surface of my mind. If Cordelia was on the boat with my aunt that afternoon, then she knew damned well that Grace was dead. Knowing this, she then made her way back to the B & B (I'm not sure how but I'll deal with that later), leaving my aunt in the water. Then she waited at the B & B as calm as spit until someone noticed that Grace didn't show up for dinner. And then what — she leaped up, hand on her heart, exclaiming, "Oh my goodness, no, she isn't here, is she?" and began the series of events that resulted in Kerry's reports. And the others — the B & B's tenants, Delia's (and Grace's) friends — what about them? Do they know this? Are they protecting Delia? Why?

The raven's back, talking to me again, and I find another french fry. "Nevermore," I say to him, just because it seems appropriate. And then I drive away very slowly down the road behind the Cloverleaf Cabins and onto 101, wondering what Kerry will have to say about our eyewitness account.

* * * * *

I'm driving carefully, keeping up with traffic, trying not to think too much about this huge *thing* that I now know, when I see brake lights ahead of me. I dutifully slow down, joining a long line of idling cars, wondering what's up. Whatever it is, it's irking me and I scan the roadside shops, wondering if anything's still open and if I can waste a little time browsing. The Indefinite Article antique shop doesn't excite me, and a restaurant named The Truculent Oyster positively depresses me but I pull over anyhow because I'm tired of breathing the exhaust of the Buick just ahead. I park, then sit in the Escort, chewing a fingernail, zoning out until I realize that the shop beside The Truculent Oyster is called Wavelengths and that it has posters of surfers, scuba divers, and snorkelers in its window. Snorkelers. *Earth to Allie — snorkelers. Yeah, yeah. Presumably they sell snorkeling gear. Someone inside may have even have sold snorkeling gear to my aunt. Big deal.* So because I have nothing to do and because I've never really examined fins and masks and whatnot, and because there's something still eating at me, I decide to venture into Wavelengths.

The Beach Boys' "Surfin Safari" is blasting as I walk through the door and I'm almost knocked down by the mingled smells of neoprene rubber, surfboard wax, and some kind of really raunchy incense that makes me wonder what the kid behind the counter is *really* burning in his incense tray. Wetsuits of varying lengths and colors hang eerily limp along one wall, reminding me of stories of the shed skins of the legendary silkies. Surfboards line the other wall, and I wander to the back of the store where there's a small display of masks, fins, and snorkels. I finger a mask, lift an amazingly heavy fin, and peer down the barrel of a snorkel. There is just no way I can imagine my aunt wearing any of this equipment but, I remind myself hastily, she did. Margaret said so.

"So, gonna do a little snorkeling?" a cheery voice inquires from behind me.

I groan. What will I have to be now — a snorkeler (about which I know zero), or a snorkeler wannabe? I opt for the latter. "Oh, I've been thinking about it," I say with unfeigned hesitation, "but all this stuff is so expensive! And I'm just, um, a beginner."

"Hey, you don't have to spend an arm and a leg," the blond, bushy-haired kid says. He's dressed in blue surfer shorts, Tevas, and a white T-shirt that says SURF TIL IT HURTS. Sure. He's got a nice tan and periwinkle blue eyes which girls must find devastatingly attractive. "Here," he says, handing me a lightweight fin made of some clear rubber-like material.

"It's light," I say, surprised. "I thought all this stuff was, you know, black and ugly."

He laughs. "You've been watching too many old Cousteau specials on TV. Nope. Snorkeling and scuba gear nowadays is cool — new materials make equipment a lot lighter and bright colors make the whole experience more awesome." He looks down at my feet. "Good feet," he says. "You could probably wear a men's size."

"Yeah, well, my family all has big feet," I mutter, pretending to consider the fin. Then, because the time seems right: "You know, a friend of mine probably bought her stuff here."

"Oh yeah?" he says, smiling, flattered.

"Uh huh, an older lady," I say, "maybe late fifties, long red hair."

He frowns, shaking his head. "I don't remember anyone like that."

I shrug. It was a long shot anyhow. "It was a couple of months ago," I tell him. "Maybe someone else was working that day?"

"Nope. I opened the store June first. To catch the tourist trade, y'know? I've been working every single day since then. Can't afford to hire help yet."

"Oh. Well, maybe I'm wrong. She probably bought it somewhere else."

"Maybe," he says. "But she would have had to go to Eugene or Portland. I'm the only water sports store on the coast."

Big deal. I guess Grace went to Eugene. So much for this bit of sleuthing. I hand him the fin, thinking how I'm going to gracefully make my exit. "I should go get her fins," I fabricate. "I want some just like hers so I'll bring them in, okay?"

"Sure," he says agreeably.

"So, has business been good?" I inquire, edging toward the door.

"Fabulous," he says. "Really, really good. Surfers, snorkelers, teenagers, little kids, you name it. A lot of women are into this. And kayakers — I sell a lot of wetsuits to them. They don't want to get wet." He chuckles. "I even sell stuff to, like, older people too. Another market segment I hadn't realized existed. You know, a bunch of ladies came in, oh, about the first of July, didn't know a thing about this stuff, but they were determined to buy snorkeling equipment."

"About the first of July?" I say, surprised. The date fit, but this was probably another "bunch of ladies" because he'd already said that Aunt Grace hadn't been in. Still, I hesitate, interested.

"Uh huh. First of July."

"But my friend — the red-haired lady — she wasn't with them?"

He shakes his head firmly. "Nah. I'd remember someone like that. I have a soft spot for redheads," he says, giving me the eye. A stray thought crosses his brain and he frowns. "The bunch that was in the first of July, they were a little, well, different. Funny."

"Oh yeah? Funny ha-ha or funny peculiar?"

"Funny peculiar. Like they were . . . embarrassed."

"They probably just felt stupid about not knowing what to buy," I suggest. "Like I do."

He shrugs. "Whatever." An impish grin steals over his face. "I shouldn't be telling you this, but the lady who tried on the fins — she had an awfully small foot, come to think of it, so I had to sell her a kid's size — she was a real fox."

"Oh yeah?" I say, feeling offended on the woman's behalf. I mean, really, here was this kid lusting after a woman probably more than twice his age!

"Yeah," he continues. "She was older, but you know, she wasn't *that* old, and she had this amazing white hair — almost silver — and these weird, gorgeous eyes and a great tan. Really cool."

I stop in my tracks. This . . . creature, this walking hormone, has just described Cordelia. "Thanks," I say, "I'll get those fins and come on back."

The door dings shut behind me and for a moment I stand on the sidewalk, in a daze. Cordelia? Buying snorkeling equipment? For my aunt? No way — the kid said he had to sell her a small fin and all us O'Neils are descendants of Bigfoot. I'm thoroughly confused. Didn't Margaret say she saw my aunt snorkeling? What gives? Dammit, none of this makes sense — every lead I turn up seems to contradict something I've just learned.

The traffic jam has cleared up and I walk back to the Escort, feeling drained. Kerry and I were both wrong thinking we needed to beat the bushes looking for an eyewitness to my aunt's death. Heck — we already had one. Cordelia. Smart move or not, I'm going to talk to her. Starting my car, I pull out into traffic, and head for Lavner Bay.

Chapter 13

I pull onto the little road leading to the B & B,
feeling angry and confused. Kerry will probably yell
at me when she finds out what I've done, but too
bad. I've decided — I'm going to confront Cordelia.
What the hell was she doing in the boat? And why
did she lie about it? Moreover, what was she doing
purchasing swim fins? An image of Cordelia showing
me the koi pool and Lorien comes unbidden to my
mind and I stuff it back into the mental compart-
ment where I'm keeping Robin's kind face and
Paula's profession of love. Gritting my teeth, I come

in sight of the B & B only to see a peculiar sight —
there's scaffolding on both sides of the front door and
plastic over the windows. Two white-overalled
painters are at work on the upper stories and a third
painter is just getting a couple more gallons out of
the back of a pickup. I park around back, noticing as
I do that there are absolutely no cars, not even Pan's
beat-up old truck, and hurry back around to the
front. What gives? The painter meets me on the
walk.

"Are you Allie?"

I note with a start two things simultaneously —
that the painter is a she and that she's wearing a
white T-shirt that says AMAZONS INC. In lavender.
Give me strength — does this mean what I think it
means? I nod yes, not trusting myself to speak. The
tall, freckle-faced young painter gives me an envelope
which she extracts from her back pocket. And a key.
"This is for you. From Cordelia. We're with the
Amazons," she grins. "We're painting the B & B.
Gotta get back to work."

I rip open the envelope.

Allie: We've taken a couple of days off. Closed
the B & B while painting is going on. You're
welcome to stay, however, if you can take care
of yourself. Or check yourself out if you like.
If you decide to stay, we'll see you Friday.
Cordelia

I grind my teeth, wad the note up into a ball,
and throw it as far as I can. Friday. This is only
Tuesday. Dammit — I want to talk to her. And I
want to talk to her now.

"Hey!" I call to the painter who gave me the note. "Excuse me — do you know where Cordelia went?"

She looks up briefly from stirring paint. "Sorry."

I'm testy now, and none too polite. "You mean if lightning struck the B & B you wouldn't know how to get ahold of her?" I can see I've hurt her feelings, but I'm still pretty riled up and frankly, Scarlett, I don't give a damn.

"I don't, but Pru might. She's up there," she says, pointing to the scaffolding. "Wanna go up?" She smiles at me wickedly.

"Hell no," I say. "I'm going inside. Maybe Pru can come in and see me when she descends from Olympus."

"Maybe," she says cheerfully. "Do you want me to ask her?"

"Please do," I say and march up the steps, heedless of paint droplets on the tarps that are covering the flagstones, and push open the front door. *You're being a butthead, O'Neil,* I tell myself as I slam the door behind me. I kick my shoes off, not wanting to get paint on the floor inside. My floor. For that matter, I guess it's my paint job and I'm suddenly mad about that, too. Who, pray tell, is paying for this? *Moi?* I don't think so.

I flop on the couch in the foyer, thinking assorted dire thoughts, counting to ten, giving myself time to calm down. Dear sweet Margaret, the self-professed stickler for accuracy, has given me, instead of answers, a whole different set of questions. Why was Cordelia in the boat with my aunt? And why did she lie about it? My theory — about a conspiracy of Cordelia's friends protecting her — suddenly seems more probable than ever. And Hormone Harry in the watersports shop has given me something else to think about — Cordelia's swim fins. For the life of me, I can't think how all this fits together. Is everyone telling the truth? Are some of them mistaken? Are some of them lying? If so, who? I stare into the dark corners of the foyer, seething, and suddenly a horrible thought occurs to me — if Cordelia really did go out in the boat with my aunt every day as Margaret asserted, then the day she died, Delia would have to have, what, abandoned my aunt at the rocks? Left her there to drown? What other explanation could fit the facts? A board creaks somewhere, and suddenly the big, quiet B & B seems oppressive — every dark corner suddenly holds a shadow and a threat. I want very badly to get back out in the sunshine. So when the front door opens, I jump a foot.

"You want to know how to get ahold of Cordelia?" a sturdy, suntanned, paint-spattered woman asks in evident exasperation.

I think fast. "Oh, well, I suppose I ought to know in case something happens while I'm staying here alone," I offer placatingly. "You know, fire, flood, earthquake."

"Hmmf," she replies. "I'll have to try to find out. Will you be here tonight?"

"Yeah. I guess so."

"I'll call you."

"Oh yeah? When?" I ask, wondering if I have to station myself in the lobby by the phone all night or only part of it.

"When I find out," the Chief Amazon informs me, turning and stomping out. So there, take that. I'm just about to formulate a pithy reply when a stray electrical impulse leaping a synapse in my none-too-reliable brain makes me remember — Kerry. And the man whose eyes want to eat something up.

"Oh, shit," I say, and lurch for the phone. Alas, Coast Investigations' line beeps busy. Grinding my teeth in frustration, I launch myself back down the steps and around the corner of the B & B to my car. She's just getting a fax, I tell myself as I gun the engine, tires chirping on the asphalt. *She's just getting a fax.*

And of course, she is. In fact, when I tear into her new office, she's wearing a fax — it's about ten feet long and she has it draped over one arm, folding it here, snipping it there.

"You're okay," I say, stating the obvious, amazed at how concerned I am. Kerry's disagreeable aunt must have really gotten to me.

"Well, yeah," she says doubtfully. "Although I was beginning to wonder if you'd forgotten about me."

"No way," I say reassuringly.

She getS stiffly to her feet. "I feel as though I'm ossified. Let me put these faxes in folders and then we can go."

"Er, go?"

"To get my truck."

Brother, talk about single-minded — I've been so engrossed with my sleuthing that I completely forgot about the fact that we're supposed to go pick up her wheels in Nautilus. Well, it's only four-thirty — with any luck, we'll make it.

"Here, take these, will you?" Kerry hands me the entire collection of filed faxes. "You can read them while I'm signing my life away for the truck."

Kerry locks up and as we make our way out into the late afternoon sunshine, I notice that she seems to be limping more than she was this morning.

"Leg hurt?" I ask.

"Yeah," she says, grimacing.

I remember the sign I saw in Robin's house: MASSAGES BY APPOINTMENT. Hell, why not? "One of the women I met today, well, she's a masseuse. Among other things."

"I'll think about it," Kerry says tersely and I decide to back off. Hey, it's her leg. "So, how did you do? Get any information."

Holy smokes — my concern for Kerry and relief at seeing that she's okay kind of swept the facts I'd found into a corner. Sometimes I wonder about myself. "Brother, did I!" I exclaim. "You wouldn't believe what these two old gals on the other side of the bay told me. Or a kid who owns the local watersports shop," and I proceed to give a precis of my findings. She listens quietly until I'm done and when she doesn't erupt in "Holy shit!" or "Egad!" or anything like that, I feel pretty deflated. "So, what do you think?" I ask.

"The old woman, Margaret, does she seem credible?" Kerry asks.

"Yeah. The kid does too. But what they had to say — they kind of contradict each other. I don't know what to think about this now. I mean, I got my question answered about my aunt really snorkeling — Margaret said she did. But then I got a new piece of information — that Cordelia was on the boat with her every time she went out. Including, of course, the afternoon she died. But the kid in the watersports store said that he sold snorkeling equipment to *Cordelia*. Not to Grace. I just can't put all the pieces together," I say in frustration. "There's something missing here."

Kerry sighs and lets her head fall back against the back of the seat. "Oh, brother."

"Oh, brother — is that a good or bad 'oh, brother'?"

"I don't know. I mean, while I was getting faxes and assembling files and all that it seemed so . . . theoretical. But you've found an eyewitness who can place Cordelia on the boat the afternoon your aunt died. The snorkeling gear, well, Allison, I just don't know. But placing Cordelia at the scene. Oh, brother," she says again.

I'm alarmed more by what's she's not saying thaN by what she is and the enormity of it all is beginning to sink in on me. I must have inadvertently slowed down to absorb all this, because the car behind me begins to honk angrily, stressing me out and making me drive even slower because I don't know where I'm going, so it's with a great sense of relief that I pull into the Toyota lot.

"Here's something else," I tell her. "On the off chance that Cordelia might just be lurking grief-stricken at the B & B, I went there just before I came to get you. And she's gone. So are the tenants."

"Gone? Gone where?"

"Dunno. The place is being painted so I'm

supposed to think that they've left to stay out of the way or out of the paint or something. I guess that means we're getting hot, right?"

She shakes her head. "I can't believe you did that. This is too serious to play around with any more, Allison. Listen, I've got to get my truck before they close. This'll just take a minute," Kerry says. "In the meantime, you can read the fax file. Then we'll go back to my place and decide what to do."

I'd like that — to decide what to do. My head feels full of bees again so there's no way I could make sense of the faxes. I don't even try. Instead, I put my seat back and stare out the window at the sky. I've always been good at puzzles but this seems to be a puzzle with too many pieces. Or pieces that don't fit together. Or maybe I'm missing a few. Or something. Before I had Margaret's information, we really had nothing but my suspicions. But now we actually have an eyewitness account — an account that contradicts the official version of events. But the fun doesn't end here. Thanks to my little visit to Wavelengths, I now have another piece of information and *that* could be interpreted as contradicting my eyewitness's account of things. I'm getting a headache just thinking about all this and hope that Kerry doesn't have in mind that we trot off to the local constabulary right away because I don't think I'm up to it. I mean, I thought I knew what the hell was going on, but now I know that I don't know.

There's a cloud going by overhead that looks an awful lot like a fish and I flash back to Delia and the koi, subtract Delia from the scene because it hurts me to remember it, and wonder suddenly who's feeding those beautiful fish. I mean they're *pets,* for cripe's sake — what kind of person would just go away and leave them? And then, because I've never been very good at keeping an orderly mind, Delia and Paula and Robin pop out of the box where I've stuffed them and I get that feeling again. Why is it that after everything I've learned, and the things I suspect, I still can't believe that Delia's a murderer. Murderess. Whatever. *And why not, pray,* my critical little pain-in-the-ass Inner Voice inquires. *You've, what, eliminated Robin from the Great Conspiracy because she has a nice cat and a kind face, Paula because she spouted some drivel about love, and Delia because she has irresistible pheromones? Some sleuth you are, O'Neil.*

I get out of my car and begin to pace. If Delia were standing here right now, what could she say to convince me that she didn't have a part in my aunt's death? Like yes, reporter Kristin got things a little wrong. Like no, she didn't go out with my aunt every day, and that no, Margaret couldn't have seen her go out with my aunt the day she drowned because she was two hundred miles away in Fish Follicle or some other such place and has a Visa receipt to prove it. And the ladies in the coffeehouse? I want Delia to tell me they were simply comforting her in her grief or weeping over the plot of the latest sappy movie.

What the hell's happening to me? I'm suffering from softening of the resolve, wilting of the will. Wanting people to be innocent who sure as hell look guilty and discounting the eyewitness testimony of a self-professed accuracy nut. And where the hell is Kerry, anyhow? I want dinner. I want to go home, or whatever passes for home, and sleep. I want my cat.

I'm tired of playing girl sleuth — did she or didn't she, is she or isn't she? I want my small, predictable life back.

A wild-eyed youth in a red Toyota truck comes roaring up the aisle between the cars, forcing me to hustle out of the way, and I give him the finger as he drives past. He gives it back to me, and I realize the vehicle he's abusing is probably Kerry's new truck. What a way for it to start its life. When I get back to the Escort, sure enough, she's waiting for me, a set of keys in her hand, a silly grin on her face.

"This is the first new car I've ever had," she says, running a hand over its fender as if it were a horse's flank. "I guess sometimes things really do turn out all right."

I'm not so sure about that but I make some encouraging noises nevertheless.

"I don't know about you, but I'm beat," Kerry says. "If you don't mind, I think I'll head on back to my room at Coast Seafoods and call it a day. I'll move into my office tomorrow, but for tonight —"

"Oops," I say, remembering the green garbage bag of personal effects that Kerry's aunt tossed at me — a bag that now reposed on the backseat of the Escort.

"We need to talk," I tell her. "And we both need to eat. There's a Chinese food place just back down the highway a bit. Let's talk there."

"Allison, I can't even think straight. I don't believe I can do any more work on the case tonight."

"That's okay," I tell her. "We need to talk about something else."

"Something else?"

"Just trust me, okay? See you there."

* * * * *

So over Kung Pao chicken and Buddhist's Delight, I tell Kerry the bad news.

"Your aunt was ... definite," I tell her. "I've got your stuff in the back of the Escort."

. I expect her to glower and scowl, a reprise of the dirty looks she was wearing when I first met her, but instead it's obvious her feelings are hurt. "She's a superstitious old lady," Kerry says. "But it's her house. She can throw me out if she likes. I guess I can sleep on the floor at my office. There ought to be a sleeping bag in all that stuff Auntie gave you."

She looks so morose that I want to reach over and pat her arm, not that that would do any good. And then I get a terrific idea. "Hey, you don't need to sleep on the floor. I own a bed and breakfast. You can come and sleep there. Cordelia and the tenants have decamped for parts unknown. They won't be back 'til the painting's done on Friday. You can probably have your pick of vacant rooms."

She looks at me doubtfully. "I could?"

"Sure," I say magnanimously, wondering if this is how my Aunt Grace got stuck with so many deadbeat tenants. Not that Kerry's a deadbeat, mind you, but she is down on her luck — just the way all the folks were who came to Lavner Bay, if Bree can be believed. Yikes — is this the way it starts?

"Okay," Kerry agrees.

"There is one more thing," I say as the waitress brings us another pot of tea. "Your aunt mentioned that a man was looking for you."

Alarm is suddenly written all over Kerry's face, and my heart lurches a little. So Auntie was right.

"She said he had 'eyes that wanted to eat something up,'" I add.

"It's that son of a bitch who tried to kill me," Kerry yells.

"Sshh, sshh, for cripe's sake," I tell her. "You'll get us thrown out of here!"

"Okay," she whispers hoarsely, "but it's him. I know it is. I caught him in the middle of my living room in Portland with a gas can. That's when he pulled the bookcase over on me. He has crazy eyes all right — he's a firebug. They're all crazy."

"But why is he looking for you? I thought the people who were after you were, well, finished with you. They torched your house and car and you got the message and got out of Dodge. No?"

Kerry looks absolutely desperate. "I don't know! I haven't the faintest idea why they still want me or how they found me, or, hell, or anything. I mean, if this is revenge, they're taking it pretty far. And what if they think I'm still there — what about the restaurant?"

"I'm sure your aunt convinced the guy that you're not there," I say with more certainty than I feel. "But, you know, it wouldn't hurt if you were to tell that kid Daniel — he says hi, by the way — to be, well, vigilant."

"You're right," she says, "it wouldn't hurt." She checks her watch. "It's suppertime. He'll be there. Let me go call him now. God, I would just die if anything happened to their business because of me. Be right back."

Sipping my tea, I try hard not to think too much about what Kerry's aunt had said — that bad luck follows her. I rub my arms nervously, suddenly feeling cold and before I have time to dwell on all this mumbo-jumbo, I'm happy to see that Kerry's back.

"Okay," she says, sliding back into the seat across from me. "Daniel's going to keep his eyes open." She swirls her tea around in her cup, fiddles with her unused chopsticks, drums her fingers on the table, and I finally get it: Kerry's a little shaken up. Maybe the best thing I could do for her is to take her to the B & B, find a bed, and put her in it.

"Well," I say breezily, "we can't sit here all night yakking our heads off. What do you say we go to Lavner Bay?"

"Allison," she says in a voice so small I can hardly hear it, "I'm scared. Before, in Portland, when I got hurt and lost everything, that was bad enough but it was only me. Here, well, there are other people involved. If anything happens to them, or their business, I'll . . . I'll . . ."

I don't quite know what to do, but I reach over and pat her hand, just a little, and to my surprise she grabs mine, holding on tight. When she opens her eyes I see how really frightened she is, and I squeeze her fingers, flashing her a confident smile. "Don't worry," I say, mouthing the world's most meaningless platitude, "things are going to be okay."

"If you say so," she says, handing over responsibility to me, and I feel the awful weight of it descend on me like Frodo's ring of power in *Lord of the Rings*. Oh man, I should have stayed in Lancaster.

"Are you okay to drive?" I ask her.

"Yeah. But let's not take 101. I'm not in shape to deal with the traffic. I'll show you a back way."

We leave money on the table to pay our bill, and I trail along behind her out into the parking lot.

"If we hurry, we can sit out on the deck and watch the sun set over Lavner Bay," I tell her. "I know where they keep the Chardonnay."

She gives me a strange look. "Follow me," she says, and I get in the Escort and pull out onto 101 after her, following as she leads me off the highway and onto a scenic, lightly traveled secondary road. *Poor Kerry,* I think as we bypass Windsock and her office, *poor unlucky Kerry,* and I hate myself for thinking this, but maybe, just maybe, Auntie was right.

Chapter 14

"So what do you think of it?" I ask Kerry as we pull up in the back of the B & B.

"Wow," she says, looking impressed, and I have to admit, it is a pretty impressive place. "What are you going to do with it?" I'm happy to see that she's regained some of her composure. Kerry as a basket case was not something I was looking forward to.

"I'm going to sell it," I tell her. "As soon as I find out what *really* happened to Aunt Grace, this place goes on the block."

"Let's take a look at the financials before you put

it up for sale," she suggests. "If it has a good cash flow, you could get a manager to run the place and draw a nice income from it."

It's on the tip of my tongue to make a rude noise and say no, but for some reason, I don't. Maybe Kerry knows what she's talking about. Maybe I could draw an income from the place — God knows, Lorien isn't making me rich. I shrug. "Okay," I tell Kerry.

Cordelia's key unlocks the back door and I lead the way, feeling like a kid trespassing on school property. The feeling kind of irritates me, so I start turning on lights, asserting my right to spend my money on electricity if I damned well want to. Kerry follows along behind me yawning, carrying her green garbage bag and the file of faxes.

"So where can I put this stuff? Do I get an ocean view?"

"I don't know," I tell her. "Presumably this key fits all the locks, so let's just start opening doors. If the room looks lived-in, we'll go on to the next."

I hadn't really noticed, but there's another room on my floor and I use Cordelia's key to open it. It's a nice room — it shares the west wall with mine and there's a bathroom which joins the rooms together. Its carpet and accents are dusty blue where mine is dusty rose, but apart from that there's the same cherrywood furniture and white chenille bedspread.

"This is okay," Kerry says. "Why don't I just dump my stuff here?"

"Go ahead and put it down," I tell her, "but let's see what else is available."

"Whatever you say," she says, looking around with interest. "Allison, this is a really nice place. Someone has taken very good care of it."

"I guess so," I say, with not very much interest, following her upstairs to the third level.

"Look at this," she says in admiration. The stairs open out onto a large open area which seems to be a library and sitting room. There's a table with a half-finished jigsaw puzzle on it, and a big-screen TV against one wall. A stone fireplace in one corner of the open area has a comfy-looking sofa in front of it. "This is great," Kerry says. "I could live here." Four doors open off this area and I pull out the key. Sure enough, it opens the first one.

"Oops," I say, looking at a little kid's mess. On the wall is a poster advertising The Fox network's quirky show, *The X Files* (THE TRUTH IS OUT THERE, the poster says) and from the ceiling hangs a model of *Star Trek*'s ship, the Enterprise. Ossie's room, I guess. As I expected, the room which adjoins it has that lived-in look too, and I guess it's Pan's.

The room on the west wall is small and, when I open it up, evidently it's Bree's — there are PETA posters on the walls, a desktop computer on a table under the window, and piles of paper everywhere. The most recent issue of *No Bad Cats* — Bree's cat behavior newsletter — is stacked on a chair just inside the door, ready to be mailed out, I guess.

The last room on this level is surprisingly large and, I suspect, belongs to the Emilys. There are flowers in vases, flower prints on the walls, and a closet full of floral dresses. I close the door quickly, feeling nauseous. So that leaves the next level.

"Really, I'm okay downstairs," Kerry says, yawning again.

"No, c'mon up," I say. "Choice is good." But, alas, there's only one room at the top of the stairs and it's occupied too. It's a funky room and I like it best because it takes up the whole top floor. Most of the ceiling is slanted, and it has neat windowseat cubbyholes built in under the gables. It is, I suspect, Cordelia's room and was, I now have to admit, my aunt's room, too. The queen-sized bed under one gabled window seems to attest to this fact, as does a photo on one bedside table of Delia and my aunt, arms around each other's shoulders, the sea in the background. Feeling like a voyeur, I step inside. I can't help myself. Stuffing my hands in my pockets, I stand awkwardly in the middle of the room, my mind a confused jumble of thoughts and impressions. My aunt lived here — probably her clothes are still in the big walk-in closet under the eaves, her books in the bookcases that stretch along one wall, her papers in one of the two desks under the window. This room is full of secrets. I could learn a lot in here. But I sure wouldn't want a stranger rummaging among my things after I'd just died — would Grace have wanted me to rummage among hers? To tell the truth, though, what's holding me back is something far more ephemeral than the respect for Grace's privacy. I shiver, finally admitting that this room is full of . . . a presence, and it's this presence that makes me reluctant to paw through my aunt's belongings. Believe me, even though I'm a purveyor of the most outlandish fantasies, I'm not one who sees ghosts or anything like that. But the presence is undeniably here — like the echo of music or the afterimage of a bright light. I rub my arms and close the door.

"I guess downstairs is it," I tell Kerry. "There seems to be no more room in the inn."

"I've just realized something," she says, following

me downstairs. "If your aunt's tenants occupy all these rooms, that only leaves the two small rooms downstairs available for tourists. How could she have profitably run this place with so little income? Well, I suppose the tenants could be paying reasonable rent —"

"I don't think so," I tell her. "The way I figure it, Grace was running a boarding house for, well, for deadbeats. From what I can gather, these ah, people, found their way here, crashed and burned, and for some reason Grace allowed them to stay on. For very little rent."

"Are you sure?"

"No, I'm not sure. But I don't think any of them have jobs or are independently wealthy. That screwy vet school dropout I told you about writes a cat behavior newsletter. How many subscribers do you suppose she has — eleven? Twelve? And the flower ladies are in perpetual la-la land and Pan is the B & B's handywoman and is probably getting free rent, and Ossie's just a kid."

"You need to get a look at the books," Kerry says. "Your aunt kept the B & B afloat somehow."

I make a snorting sound. "Kerry, I could look at the books from now 'til Christmas and I wouldn't know what I'm looking at. Or for. I'm not good with . . . that kind of structured record-keeping."

"But you have a business," she says reasonably.

"Sure. But my record-keeping for Lorien is, um, marginal. Yeah, marginal's a good word. I have this spiral notebook, see — one without lines, I can't do lines — and I just enter what I pay out and what I take in and kind of total everything up now and then." Seeing her evident horror, I shrug. "You see?"

"What about your taxes?"

"My friend Bradley does them for me. He tells me how much to write a check for and I do."

"Typical right-brained behavior," Kerry says. "Let's hope it isn't hereditary." She sighs. "I'll take a look at the B & B's books for you."

"You will? That's great."

"Tomorrow, though. I'm going to bed now," she says, opening the door to the blue room and tossing her garbage bag inside.

"Okay. I'm going to find that Chardonnay and sit on the deck," I tell her. "So don't be alarmed if you hear noises."

"Nothing could alarm me because I'll be asleep. Don't worry." She closes the door to her room, leaving me alone in the hallway where I feel silly. So I decide to go on into my room with the fax file and read for a while before I set out in search of the Chardonnay. I flop on the bed, peruse the file for about three minutes before I set it aside and just listen. From my room, I can hear Kerry moving around in hers, taking a shower, putting things in drawers, and I'm suddenly happy that I'm not here completely alone or alone among Delia and the gang. Even though Kerry isn't exactly a friend, she isn't exactly a stranger, and this thought pleases me. I yawn, thinking about friendship and family and Kerry's aunt and my aunt when I'm suddenly so tired that I can't think about anything except *Did I lock the door*? I don't get to answer the question before sleep overtakes me.

Chapter 15

Suddenly, it's morning — six-thirty to be exact — and I'm amazed that I slept through the night without waking, cuddled up to the file of faxes. Coffee, I think, I need coffee, and stumble out of bed to the bathroom, yawning and stretching. I splash some water on my face, run a comb through my hair, study my reflection, and come to a reluctant conclusion. *You scare people,* I tell my image. *That's why they've been looking at you like you're a Klingon. You've got to tone things down if you don't want to ruffle people's feathers — for instance, don't flash your tattoo. Sure, it's just a black cat like Sammy, and sure it's on your shoulder, but people are easily upset. And maybe you should have the color taken out of your hair — return to the O'Neil red. You might think about wearing something different too. Your ripped jeans and gloomy T-shirts are not cutting it here in conservative Oregon.* I peer at myself with interest — what would I look like with the trademark O'Neil red hair again, maybe cut into something short and stylish? And yeah, I don't have to exactly *display* my tattoo. Also, what if I dressed in something non-threatening like Kerry? Yikes. I'd be a Normal Person. At least on the outside. Now there's a really scary thought. I step out into the hall and almost run into my investigator friend who's scrubbed and shiny and already dressed in a preppy-looking blue chambray shirt and khakis. Nah, I decide, I'm not the preppy type, but I could pick up a pair of Levi's. And maybe a flannel shirt. I've noticed a lot of flannel women here on the coast — must be some kind of regional costume. I have a tiny moment of panic realizing that I'd be donning yet another disguise, assuming yet another persona, but the moment passes and I'm fine. Well, not quite fine — I do need some coffee. Kerry, I note, has a steaming mug of something in her hand.

"What's that?" I ask hopefully.

"Coffee. I found the kitchen and the coffeemaker and a fridge full of stuff. I'm assuming we can help ourselves — to breakfast, anyhow."

I shrug, wondering about the propriety of it before I remember that hey, I *own* this place. "Sure we can," I tell her.

"Downstairs and back through the lobby," Kerry says. "I left some coffee in the pot."

I'm in the middle of thawing some muffins in the microwave and making another pot of coffee when I hear a vehicle come driving far too fast up the little road beside the B & B. *Crazy women painters,* I mutter, pulling open the window and sticking my head out to tell them to cool it. But it isn't Amazons, Inc., it's Kerry's cousin Daniel, barefoot, wearing only a white tank top, something that looks suspiciously like baggy green plaid flannel boxer shorts, and a worried frown. I guess grim looks run in the Owyhee family. He sees me at the window and yells. "Kerry? Is she here?"

"Yeah," I tell him. "Come in. The door's probably unlocked." What gives, I wonder.

"Oh jeez, oh jeez," he says, practically falling into the kitchen. "Have you heard?"

"Heard what?" I say, wondering for one awful moment if Auntie has departed this earth.

"Heard what?" Kerry asks, appearing in the kitchen doorway behind me. "What's wrong? It's not the restaurant, is it?'"

"No, no," he says, running a hand over his buzz cut. "That place you told me you rented, you know, when you called me last night, well it's gone. Torched. Burned to the ground. I was there and it's toast. Talk about luck that you decided to spend the night here. Can I have some coffee?" he asks me, and I point to the pot.

"Oh, dammit!" Kerry yells, sitting down heavily at the kitchen table. "Everything I own . . . all my new business equipment . . . it wasn't even insured yet!"

"The guy who did it, it's the guy who came looking for you yesterday, isn't it?" Daniel asks. "The guy who got Ma so rattled that she tossed your stuff out?"

Kerry nods.

"So who is he, Ker?"

"Oh, hell, I don't know. Probably the same guy who burned my place in Portland. But how did he find me here?"

"Sounds like you're in a lot of trouble if you have, like, arsonists or whoever chasing you."

"I thought I'd be safe coming here," she says. "But now I see I won't be."

"So what'd you do to him?" Daniel asks.

"I didn't do anything to *him*. I found out some information that put a crooked contractor out of business and I guess the jerk just can't let go of it. He hired this . . . firebug to scare me out of town, or so I thought. But now I'm not so sure. If he's still after me —"

"Then he wants to do more than scare you. This is too cool," Daniel exclaims.

"I'm awfully glad you think so," Kerry says, giving him a glare.

"No, I mean, listen. There's more and that's what's cool. Last night I stayed awake watching the restaurant but then I thought what about your new place so I sent Kenny over with my cell phone. About three a.m. he calls me to say someone's snooping around. I tell him to lie low, you know, not take any chances, and when I get there — it couldn't have taken me more than five minutes — the main building is on fire. Ker, there was nothing I could do — it went up like a bomb had exploded inside. I find Kenny in the bushes and we call nine-one-one and beat it out of there. Then I call Uncle George and he shows up in his truck and we're, like, hiding, wondering what to do, watching the fire from the parking lot of the store across the road when we see this car parked in the bushes by the real estate company. Kenny just about has a fit and when we get him calmed down he tells me it's the car the guy came in, the guy who burned your place down! I ask him is he sure and he says yes he is, so George and I get out and go through the bushes and come out on either side of the guy's car and well, we just get in with him."

"Omigod, Daniel," Kerry says weakly.

"No big deal," Daniel says modestly. "George puts his hand around the guy's throat and we get him down on the seat and stuff one of my socks in his mouth and tie him up with my shirt and George's belt. Then we just kind of carry him back to my truck, no problem, because he's such a skinny little guy. We sit him up beside Kenny who says yeah, that's him, and George just grunts. In a minute he smiles and says to follow him and so we drive out of there nice and quiet and slow."

"Where is he?" Kerry says, an I'm-going-to-kill-him look in her eyes.

"We've got him," Daniel says. "I can take you to him if you want."

"Why would I want you to take me to him?" she says. "Let's call the police and give him to them."

"Yeah, okay, we can do that," Daniel says, "but just listen a minute."

"Listen to what?" Kerry asks, suspicious.

"What will happen to him? You know about this stuff."

The cousins look at each other, Kerry calms down, and when she answers him, there's ice in her voice. "He'll be arrested. If the D.A. thinks there's enough evidence — and we have only the word of a ten-year-old Indian boy — charges will be brought against him. Chances are he'll make bail." She's quiet for a moment. "If he's smart, he'll press charges against you and George for kidnapping and false imprisonment," Daniel blushes at this, "or file a civil suit, but he's probably not going to want to stick around for that. My feeling is that he'll disappear. For a while."

"Yeah," Daniel says, "for a while."

Kerry looks at Daniel again and it's as though there's telepathy between the two of them, they're so intense. I sense there's something important going on here, some decision Kerry has to make, and when she finally speaks, it's obvious she's made it. "You said you've got him. Where is he?" she asks.

"On Indian land."

Kerry exhales. "Who knows?"

"The family. The tribal elders."

"You're going to do something to him, aren't you? What?"

"Keep him for a while. Talk to him. Pray over him."

"Pray over him?" Kerry says scornfully.

Daniel smiles. "We have our own ways of doing things. The man — he'll have to participate in a ceremony of atonement. Uncle George explained it to me. He'll be required to give back the things he took from you. Then, after he's done that and is truly contrite, he'll ask you for your forgiveness."

"He'll ask me — you mean I have to be there?"

"Yes. At the end. To face him."

"I don't know if I can do that, Daniel. Let me think about it. Okay?"

Daniel shakes his head. "No. Either you want the tribe's help or you don't. If you don't, Kenny and I will drive the guy into the bush and let him go. But if you do . . ."

"How long will this . . . ceremony take?"

"Several days. Maybe a week."

"And this will . . . finish things between us?"

Daniel smiles again and it's not a pleasant smile. "Yes."

They both turn and look at me for the first time since this weird conversation began, realizing belatedly that I'm not just another kitchen chair. "I . . . excuse me," I say, getting the message, grabbing my coffee mug, and preparing to flee outside onto the deck.

"Allison, don't go," Kerry says, sounding desperate, putting a hand on my arm.

"You've heard everything anyhow," Daniel says. "It's a little late to run."

"Oh brother," I say, sitting back down, gulping my cold coffee. I mean, what they're calmly discussing may be an ancient and meaningful Indian ceremony but it's still vigilante justice, for cripe's sake.

"All right," Kerry tells Daniel.

"Okay," Daniel says, getting up. "I'll go let Uncle George know."

"Fine," Kerry says, sounding dazed. Then: "Wait. Does your mother know about this?"

Daniel nods.

"Oh," Kerry says, a pathetic note of hope in her voice. "And she agreed? To help me?"

"No. She was outvoted."

Kerry looks away and I feel immediately sorry for her. But that brings something to mind, something Daniel's mother said, and I call to him, just as he's about to leave. "Hey, Daniel, what's a *na-set*?"

He looks back at me, a strange expression on his face, but not half as strange as the expression on Kerry's face. "How do you know about the *na-set*?" he asks.

"Remember yesterday in the restaurant? Your mother mentioned it, ah, in passing."

"Oh yeah, she did, didn't she?"

Kerry looks from Daniel to me. "What are you two talking about?"

"Go ahead," I tell Daniel. "If you know, tell her. After all, it's what this stupid feud is all about. Isn't it?"

Daniel leans against the doorframe, looking at Kerry.

"Daniel?" Kerry says tentatively.

"Yeah, okay," he agrees. "As far as I know it, here's the story. Your mother, Alva, was like the family's favored daughter." He rubs his hair again. "It's kinda long and complicated. Our tribe has this ritual and I know you probably don't know anything about it and will think it's silly but the tribe doesn't and my mom doesn't either."

"Go on," Kerry says quietly.

"Okay. So anyhow, the ritual is called *nay-dosh* — well, it's a ceremony really — and it's one of the Feather Dances and it's a pretty big deal. In the last century hundreds of our people were massacred by the whites just for holding *nay-dosh*. They killed them in the dance houses and those who managed to escape outside were slaughtered in the dirt. Nice, huh? All our regalia — the costumes and so on that had been passed down from father to son and mother to daughter — were destroyed. It's not like the Feather Dances are war dances or anything like that." He laughs. "They're peaceful things, see, and this one is held on the shortest day of the year and celebrates renewal. That's what *nay-dosh* means — world renewal. It's held to send our thanks to the Creator."

"And the *na-set*?" Kerry asks.

"Oh yeah. Well, the *na-set* is, like, a woman's wealth. It's a bunch of stuff sewn onto a buckskin dress — dozens of necklaces of gemstones and hard clamshells and beads, and otter skins and mink, and things like that. Really, the *na-set is* the dress, I guess." He clears his throat nervously. "And the dress, well, it's supposed to sing with happiness when the women dance."

"And my mother?" Kerry asks grimly.

"Took the *na-set* when she left."

"Oh no," Kerry says. Then: "Was it hers?"

"Not exactly," Daniel says. "The Feather Dance, well, we're just learning how to do it again, and how to make the regalia, and all the women worked on that *na-set*. So it really belonged to our family and was, like, quite a blow when your mother took it."

I remember that Daniel's mother said she heard the dress cry when it was stolen and I swallow nervously. Well, maybe she did. If these people can hold a ceremony to make an arsonist sorry then who's to say that they can't make a dress that cries and sings?

"My mother — it upset her a lot," Daniel says. "She's old-fashioned and the old way is that the *na-set* needs to be taken outside between dances and hung up and it will, ah, dance by itself. They believe it cries if it doesn't get to dance."

"Oh God," Kerry says. "What a thing to do. Why did she do it?"

Daniel shrugs. "The sisters argued. Over your mother's choice of man, Uncle George says. Maybe she took the *na-set* as revenge."

"Or maybe she took it to remember her people," I suggest, not wanting Kerry's mom to be the heavy here.

"Whatever. But she shouldn't have done it," Kerry says gloomily. She looks hopefully at Daniel. "Is there anything, I mean, there must be something I can do to make things right. Is there?"

"Make another *na-set*," Daniel says. "My mom's too mad and proud to make one and the family doesn't have any other girls. So our family doesn't have women to dance in the Feather Dance."

"She's that mad? After all these years?"

"After all these years."

"Well then, I guess I have to do it," Kerry says. "I'll make another one."

Daniel is amazed. "You will?"

"I will. But only if your mother will help me. After all, she helped with the other one, right?"

"Right," he says slowly.

"And I certainly don't know how to make one."

"Right," he says again, thinking. "But you'll have to ask her yourself. For her help."

"Oh God," Kerry says, looking desperate. "How can I do that?"

"I don't know," Daniel says, shrugging. "You'll have to figure that out. And I hope you can — figure it out, I mean — because it's a good idea. Right now, though, I have to leave. See you in a couple of days. Will you be here?"

Kerry looks at me.

"What? Yeah, sure," I say. "We'll be here."

And he's gone.

"I need a drink," Kerry says after the sound of Daniel's truck has died away. "But it's too early in the day." She looks at her watch. "It's only eight a.m. and already I've been an accessory to multiple offenses. Let's see: withholding evidence, false arrest, kidnapping, probably assault —"

"More coffee?" I suggest brightly.

"My God, Allison, can you believe that?"

I bustle around, making more coffee. "Which 'that'? The stuff about what they're going to do to the arsonist or the bit about the dress?"

"Either. Both."

"I guess. Why not?"

"Why not? Because I'm a logical person, that's why not. Because . . . oh, hell, I don't know why not."

"Coffee," I say, handing her a fresh cup. "Seeing as how you're asking my opinion, here it is: I think you're pretty darned lucky."

"Lucky? Why?"

"Kerry, think about it. You've got a family, hell, you've got a whole tribe that's going to go to bat for you. And you've got a chance to make amends. You've got something to belong to. A family. If you want it."

She's silent, looking into her coffee mug.

"Well, do you want it?"

"Yeah, I do," she says, looking up.

"Then do what Daniel said. Make another dress."

"I haven't the faintest idea where to start."

"Ask someone. You'll get a new computer — didn't Daniel say they'll make the arsonist repay you — so put your request out on the Internet. You'll have a dozen replies by lunch, I bet."

She brightens at this. "I could do that."

"Sure you could."

She's quiet for a bit, evidently thinking about her melted electronics equipment. "I guess I better call the rental agent," she says finally. "Maybe she can claim my business equipment when she files with her insurer." But she doesn't make a move toward the phone. Perhaps her blood sugar is low.

"How about a muffin?" I ask. She doesn't answer, and I start to get alarmed. "Earth to Kerry," I say, giving her arm a little shake.

"Sorry," she says, coming back to reality. "I was just thinking."

"Yeah? What about?"

"About the fact that maybe the universe is sending me a message."

Oh, oh. This sounds dire. "Oh? What kind of message?"

"That maybe my dream of coming here and starting a business — and yes, I'll admit it, of somehow being accepted by my family and taken back into the tribe — isn't meant to happen. This is all so *hard.*" She wipes a hand angrily across her face and my alarm turns to panic. She's crying and I'm terrible with people who cry. I never know what to do — offer them a Kleenex, ignore their tears, hug them — so I do nothing but bite my lip and worry. "I was a fool for thinking things might turn out — things usually don't. Dammit! Hell!" she yells and I realize these are probably the strongest cuss words that well-brought-up Kerry knows. A wild look comes into her eyes. "You know," she says to me, "I'm tempted to throw my stuff into my truck and just . . . take off. Go. Get out of here. Leave all this behind."

For one giddy instant, I'm tempted to ask her if I can come along. I get this image of the two of us cruising the country in Kerry's Toyota Tacoma, not a care in the world, but the image pops like a bubble as common sense prevails. "You can't just take off," I tell her reasonably. "You already told Daniel to start the whatever it is that they're going to do to the guy who torched your place."

She clearly doesn't want to be reasoned with because she yells something incomprehensible at me and pounds the table. That's when I decide to clear out and let her cry or scream or whatever she needs to do to get this out of her system. "Well, I'm going to take a shower," I tell her, just to let her know she hasn't offended me or anything and, nice and calm, I pour myself another mug of coffee, hoping that when I come back, she won't have zoomed off in the Tacoma for parts unknown, leaving me to explain to Daniel that's she cut and run and, worse yet, to sort through *my* problems alone which, alas, I don't think I can run away from.

So I shower, shampoo, blow-dry, and don the least threatening garb I possess — a plain white T-shirt and a pair of unripped black Levi's — when I hear a tentative knock at the door. Hoping it's Kerry, I open up and sure enough, here she is — eyes red and puffy, but here nonetheless.

"I thought you were taking off," I say, just to test the waters.

She shakes her head. "No. I've been coming back here — in my mind, that is — ever since I can remember. I'm staying."

"So you're going to show up for the ceremony of atonement or whatever it is and find out how to make a new dress?"

She nods.

"Atta girl. What about the rest of it. What about your business? Coast Investigations?"

"I don't know about that," she says. "I'll finish your case and then . . . reassess things. I'm certainly not going to open another office anytime soon. It may sound wimpy, but before I can help other people I need to feel . . . safe."

"I understand," I tell her, finally seeing how fragile she really is. Her love of logic and order, her fondness for her files and computers — she's arranged things so that she stays at arm's length from life. I feel a moment of pity for her and then I have this revelation: who am I to pity her? With my mail order business, and my funny, baggy clothes, and my hermit-like existence, how am I any different from Kerry? We've just erected different defenses to keep life at bay.

"I can always do something else," she continues. "Find a job. Go back to the gaming center, maybe."

"Sure," I say encouragingly. "There are lots of possibilities."

"But we need to wind things up on your case first. So," she says, "I thought we might talk over how to proceed. Figure out what we already know and what we need to know and how to get there. If you like."

"Sure," I say again. "You're the boss. Give me a minute and I'll come down to the kitchen. Is that okay?" I realize I'm being as solicitous of her as she is of me, but I guess that's all right.

"I put on some more coffee," she says, not meeting my eyes.

Oh God, not more coffee. I'll be bouncing off the ceiling. "Great," I enthuse. "Let me get the faxes and I'll be right down."

I close the door, rooting around in my stuff for some clean socks, saying a small prayer of thanks that Kerry didn't just take off. Despite the fact that she said yes to Daniel, and despite her half-hearted hopes for reconciliation, she really has no ties here. In her place, I might well have split. But maybe that's one of the differences between us — she's what, honorable? So what does that make me?

She's sitting at the kitchen table, a yellow legal pad in front of her, the top page neatly divided into two columns. There's some notes already made on the page, I see. When I sit down, she looks up, all business. "Here we'll put down what we know and here we'll list what we need to know," she says. Flipping the page, she shows me the heading MOM.

"What's MOM?"

"Motive, opportunity, and method," she says.

"Oh yeah," I say, recalling such jargon from the books I sell.

"So we presume what's happened is murder, right?"

When I say nothing, she looks up at me. "Allison? We are still presuming it's murder, aren't we?"

I rake my hair with one hand. "Yeah. I mean, I guess so. Sure. What else could it be?"

Putting down her pencil, she looks at me with frank curiosity. "You sound . . . doubtful. Did you find something you're not telling me about?"

"No. I didn't find anything . . ."

"But?"

"But what?"

"There's an implicit 'but' in what you were saying," Kerry says. "You need to tell me what it is."

"I don't know what it is," I tell her. "Just a feeling, dammit." There, I've said it. "That we're on the wrong track."

She looks at me skeptically.

"I know, I know. There are only two choices, right. Did she jump or was she pushed?"

Kerry frowns, shocked, I guess, by my levity. "The example you just gave is such an old chestnut that it's a cliché. And actually, it's quite misleading," she says fussily. "She could have jumped, been pushed, slipped, had a heart attack — the list of possibilities is, well, it's long. What happened to your aunt seems to have fewer explanations, so it's not necessarily a good parallel."

"Okay, okay," I say. "I was just trying to lighten things up." I wave my hand at the yellow tablet. "Let's do it. Write down what we know and all that."

Kerry nods. "Okay. We know a lot of technical stuff — from the accident report and so on and I've already written that down. Time of death, cause of death, condition of the body — that sort of thing. Now we need to add what your eyewitness said — that Cordelia always went out in the boat with Grace and that the boat didn't necessarily go out every day. Right?"

"Right."

"And we need to add what the boy in the water sports store said — that Cordelia bought fins."

"Uh huh. And that she had a bunch of women with her."

"Did he say anything about the women? Were they, for instance, the people who live in the B & B?"

I shake my head. "I don't think so. He was so fixed on Cordelia it would have taken someone like Madonna to make a greater impression on him, the little germ. But he wouldn't have referred to Bree and Pan as 'older women,' would he? Because they're not. Well, they're older than him, but they're not *older* older, if you know what I mean. So I'm assuming they were Cordelia's friends — the ones I saw her with at the coffeehouse."

"And they are?"

"The women I told you about. The ones I tried my recently deceased relative act on." I sigh.

"I remember. The ones you thought were guilty of something but not your aunt's murder."

"Yeah."

She puts her pencil down. "What do you think they're guilty of, Allison?"

"Okay, well, it's not thinking. I have no logical basis for it so it's a feeling, right, and I *feel* they know how my aunt died. But I also *feel* they weren't involved in it."

"Because they're, what, too nice?"

I'm squirming now. "Well, yeah. Among other things."

"Nice people can be murderers, too," Kerry suggests gently.

"I know that — I've thought about that — but none of them except Cordelia had anything to gain," I say bleakly. "And I can hardly see *her* knocking off my aunt for a measly ten grand. I mean, if everyone who got money from Grace's estate is a suspect, then we might as well consider Ossie. And the Emilys, for cripe's sake."

Kerry flips the page. "And they're conveniently absent, aren't they."

I sigh. "Yeah, they are."

"Okay, let's leave the nice friends for a moment and get back to method, opportunity, and motive," Kerry says. "Opportunity is usually easiest. Let's start there. Who knew about your aunt's snorkeling?"

I shrug. "Who didn't know? Her friends — Robin and Paula and the others — they knew. I'm assuming they were the ones helping Cordelia buy fins. I'm assuming, too, that they went out on the Fourth of July to have a party on the Whaler. And Grace's tenants knew."

Kerry looks up from her writing. "Okay, they all knew, but knowledge isn't the same as opportunity. Let's think now about who had the *opportunity* to murder your aunt?"

I consider this. "According to Margaret, Cordelia was the only one she ever saw on the boat. Besides my aunt."

"Okay," Kerry says. "Cordelia had opportunity. And she had a motive — the money."

"Oh, c'mon. Really?"

Kerry shrugs. "If you like, let's get Cordelia's credit report. That ought to show us something." When I say nothing, she adds, "People have killed for less."

I think about Cordelia with the koi and shake my head, but I know it's true. People in the books I sell kill for a lot less. "Okay," I agree. "We've got motive and opportunity."

"The method has me a little stumped, though," Kerry says. "Assuming Cordelia went out in the boat with your aunt the day she killed her, how did she arrange it that your aunt just . . . drowned." I put my head in my hands and Kerry says, "I'm sorry. Is this too upsetting for you?"

"No," I say. "Let's go on. Maybe she held her head underwater or fended her off with an oar. Or upped anchor and moved the boat."

Kerry's chewing the end of the pencil. "Allison, how did Cordelia get back to the B & B?"

I sit up straight, realizing that Kerry's put her finger on something that's been bugging me. How *did*

Cordelia get back? She didn't get back on the Whaler because it was still anchored out at the rocks. "Either she swam back — dammit, maybe that's what she bought swim fins for — or someone came and got her." Then I get up to pace. "God, now we're talking about a conspiracy, aren't we, with Cordelia's friends involved. And all this . . . plotting for ten grand?" I'm agitated now, really agitated. Maybe I'm wrong. Maybe those nice women are in this up to their teeth. But all of them? For cripe's sake, this is beginning to look like *Murder on the Orient Express*.

Kerry scribbles, then looks up. "You know, maybe Cordelia thought more was at stake." She chews her pencil again. "But that seems unlikely — after all, she was only the B & B's manager. If Grace died without a will — say in a drowning accident — her estate would pass to her family."

I can see I'm going to have to spill the beans. "What you suggested — it doesn't seem so unlikely. I think Cordelia and my aunt were . . . lovers."

"Oh," Kerry says in a funny voice, as though she's embarrassed. "I see. What makes you think that?"

"Some things Bree said. And the kid in the coffeehouse mentioned that everyone knew Cordelia and Grace were close. Ha! And . . . there's a photo upstairs. They have their arms around each other."

"So if Cordelia didn't know about you, she might well have assumed she'd inherit the B & B."

I nod. "So she staged her lover's drowning, got a few friends not only to lie for her but to help her, and figured she was home free?" I bite a hangnail in distress. "Is that what we're talking about?"

"And then you showed up."

"Yeah, but she doesn't know that I'm me."

"Of course she does," Kerry says. "She ran away, didn't she?"

"Yeah, she did. Allie Grace wasn't the cleverest of aliases, was it? But I was under pressure. I had an eleven-year-old waiting for an answer."

"Don't be too hard on yourself. No matter what name you used, once Cordelia checked your credit card, she'd know who you were."

I sigh. "True."

"So we can assume that Cordelia knows that you're you and that you're suspicious and that's why she and the tenants are gone. She's in a panic. The painting is a cover-up."

Speaking of painters, judging by the sounds of loud music, laughter, and engines, the Amazons have arrived.

"My head hurts," I tell Kerry. "I'm all 'what-iffed' out."

"You know what we ought to do, don't you?"

"Yeah," I say, "I do. Hand this over to the police then go get drunk in some nice, quiet, dark beachside bar."

I'm silent, actively considering this option, when Kerry asks a question. "Where is Cordelia?"

"I haven't a clue. The head Amazon outside could tell you." She looks at me oddly and I explain. "It's the business that's painting this place. Amazons, Inc."

She gets up and marches smartly out into the lobby and I hear the front door bang shut behind her. I stare at the kitchen wall, zoning out, dreading even the thought of talking to the local cops when Kerry comes back, waving a piece of paper. "Got it," she says. "That Pru person was really quite agreeable

181

once I told her I was an insurance investigator and needed just a minute of Cordelia's time before I recommended that she be awarded the full six thousand dollars that was claimed for the recent kitchen fire."

"You're amazing," I tell her. "But what's the 'it' you got?"

"Cordelia's phone number. C'mon."

"Where are we going?"

"The phone company. We're going to use the reverse directory. That'll tell us where she is. Then we're going to pay her a visit."

"A...but I thought you said we ought to hand this over to the police?"

"No, Allison, that's what you said."

"Oh, did I? But it's the reasonable thing to do, isn't it? I mean we've got method, opportunity, and motive. Now let's let the professionals handle it. Right?"

"I know it's the reasonable thing to do. But you'll never be happy unless you talk to Cordelia. Hear what she has to say, no matter how improbable it may sound. Isn't that what you want to do — talk to her?"

"Yeah, I do. And then?"

"And then we can hand her over to the police."

I consider this. "Okay. But we'd better not both walk in and confront her. I mean, no one knows about this stuff," I gesture at the yellow tablet where we've scribbled our speculations, "but us."

Kerry rips the pages off her yellow legal tablet and rummages in the B & B's kitchen drawers, finally producing an envelope and a stamp.

"What are you doing?" I ask her.

"Addressing this to Daniel. I'll mail it when we go to the phone company. It's our insurance. If Cordelia cudgels us to death with her swim fins, then Daniel will give this to the police." She frowns. "Actually he and Uncle George will probably come looking for Cordelia themselves, but that won't be my problem." Kerry has a manic glint in her eyes and I must admit, I don't feel terrifically well-balanced myself. We've both slipped a cog somewhere along the way because who in their right minds would trip off so insouciantly to question a murderer? Murderess. Whatever.

"Okay," I agree. "Let's go find Cordelia."

Chapter 16

It's laughable, really. I mean, Kerry didn't even
need the reverse directory. It seems Cordelia and the
gang are holed up at the Cloverleaf Cabins —
Numbers 4, 5, and 6. Hell, we could have walked.
We're in Kerry's Toyota, driving along the little road
behind the cabins, Lavner Bay on our right, and I'm
so nervous I can hardly sit still.

"Maybe they're out," I suggest as Kerry pulls the
truck off the road.

"And maybe they're not." When I make no move to get out, she urges, "C'mon. Let's go."

"Okay, okay, give me a minute." I take a look at the rocks off Lavner Bay to try and pump some indignation or anger or something into my system. But all I feel is sadness. *Why, you're sad, aren't you?* the perceptive Robin had asked. Yeah. I guess I am.

The little bay is flat and blue and perfect this morning. At the landward end, where a small river drains into the bay, there's a sand beach with a watercourse cut into it, and about a jillion seagulls are standing in the fresh water, wings folded contentedly, zoned out on seagull dreams. A sleek black head pops up just at the surfline and a spotted sea lion hauls itself awkwardly onto the sand. I have a moment of anxiety on his behalf until I realize that there's absolutely no one around to harass him. He finds a spot to his liking and settles down for a snooze. On the bay's far shore, my aunt's — no, my — Bed and Breakfast sits gray and solid like some kind of enormous sea creature come to land, perhaps to guard the entrance to the bay. *Enough fantasy,* I tell myself and get out of the truck, slamming the door. *No more personae, no more pretending. There's just me — Allison Grace O'Neil.*

"I hoped you'd come," a voice says from behind me and I don't have to turn around to know it's Delia. She's dressed in white pants and a pale yellow T-shirt and looks, well, dammit, she looks terrific.

"Who are you?" Kerry says suspiciously, coming around from the driver's side of the Tacoma.

"Cordelia Norville, Kerry Owyhee," I say, making introductions.

185

"Ah," Kerry says, surprise in her voice. "Cordelia. I thought you'd be . . . older."

"Allison — you want to talk to me, don't you?" Delia says.

All I can do is nod my head.

"Let's go down to the beach. We can walk along the sand to those driftwood logs over there."

I look at Kerry. "Okay," she says.

Delia smiles. "Is this your guardian angel?" she asks me.

"I'm a private investigator," Kerry tells her testily. "Allison thinks she needs to talk to you before we go to the police. I'm not in favor of it, but . . ." She lets the word hang in the air. "I'll wait here on the bank," she tells me. "You should be in sight the whole time. Be careful."

"Okay," I say, finally finding my voice.

"This way," Delia says and I'm astounded to see that she's not at all concerned. At least she doesn't seem to be. I follow her down a little path to the sand. When I look behind me, I see Kerry, a comforting presence. "Poor Allison," Delia says to me. "I'm not going to eat you up."

We walk out to where the sand is still wet from the outgoing tide and when Delia turns to me, all I can think of is how beautiful she is with her silver hair and her pale eyes and what a sap I am for even coming here when I should have gone directly to the cops who would, one presumes, be immune to whatever it is I'm feeling.

"Grace and I were lovers," she says, "if that's one of the things you want to know."

I swallow, suddenly shy. "Yeah. It is."

"But I don't want to direct this conversation. Ask the questions you came here to ask."

I can't help it. I have to know and I can't think of a good way to ask the question so I just ask it. "Why did you do it?"

She looks at me and I see in her eyes what I saw the afternoon I first met her, when she told me that a friend of hers had put the Lorien plaque by the koi pond. I had thought it was just sadness, but now I see it was grief. "Why did I do what? Kill Grace? That's what you think I did, don't you?"

"Yes. I do."

She smiles. Just a little. "Grace said you'd probably think that."

I feel myself slipsliding away from reality and close my eyes to get a grip on things. One of us is loony here and for once I don't think it's me. "Right," I say. "When you discussed killing my aunt with her, she said, what, that I'd come around asking questions and after I'd gathered all the facts, I'd conclude that you'd done it?"

"That's pretty much what she said, yes," Delia tells me.

I take a deep breath. "Okay. I'm here. I came, gathered facts, and now I'm accusing you. I think you killed her."

"I loved her," Delia says. "Why would I have killed her?"

"For the ten grand you were going to inherit."

She laughs, but there's no amusement in her voice. "I don't need ten thousand dollars."

"Don't hand me that," I scoff. "Everyone needs ten thousand dollars."

"Listen to me," Delia says. "I, and almost every one of my friends, came here seeking to simplify our lives. When I left Washington, I paid off all my bills, sold my house, gave away my furniture. I pared things down. Money? I have more than enough money. I don't need ten thousand dollars."

"So you're going to find a charity and give it away, right?"

"I'm tempted to do so," she says. "But Grace wanted me to have it, so I might not."

This is all too improbable for me. What is she, an ascetic? I mean, my life is practically pared to the bone and I can think of dozens of ways to use ten thousand dollars. I see I'm not going to get anywhere with this line of questioning, so I try another.

"Tell me what happened on the Whaler that day," I ask her. There. That ought to do it.

"No," she says, surprising me. "I won't." She closes her eyes and when she opens them, they're wet with tears. "Not like this. Not because you're angry and you demand it. Knowing is not your right."

There it is, then. "Fine," I say. "Then you're going to tell the police. Ten grand or no ten grand, I believe you killed my aunt. You're the only one with motive and opportunity. As for exactly what happened," I make myself laugh scornfully, "well, the police will eventually get it out of you."

She says nothing, just stands there looking at me, tears spilling down her cheeks.

"You're pathetic," I tell her, getting wound up now, a rage I didn't know I possessed bubbling up from somewhere inside. "And your friends are too. To kill someone you love, someone who's your friend, for money? Hell, she left you the money in her will. You would have had it eventually. Why did you have to kill her?"

Still she says nothing and, disgusted, I turn and walk back toward Kerry. I was wrong to have come here. This woman is a fruitcake, but not a charmingly eccentric one as I first thought. No, instead she's a dangerous, off-her-rocker fruitcake. So when she catches up with me, grabbing me by one arm and spinning me around, I can't help it. I mean, I'm scared, right, so I grab the front of her shirt with one hand and make a fist with the other, preparing to deck her.

"You stupid . . . girl!" she screams at me. "I didn't kill Grace. She killed herself!"

Chapter 17

We're sitting in the sand, the three of us (Kerry had come limping down the bank and out onto the beach when she saw Cordelia chase me), talking quietly, and I'm feeling pretty bad. All the pieces that didn't fit before, well, they're fitting now.

"So how long had she been ill?" Kerry asks.

"About six months. The tumor behind her eye just kept growing. They'd tried a laser treatment on it once but the procedure was so painful that Grace asked them to stop midway."

I feel sick. "You mean she was conscious?"

"Yes. She had to be."

"And they couldn't operate?" Kerry asks, suspicious to the end.

"No. She'd already lost the sight in one eye. If they operated to remove the tumor, they would have had to remove the other eye. And the tumor was malignant. She felt — and her doctors agreed — that they would just be buying her time. But what kind of time?" Delia shakes her head. "Grace didn't want to spend her last days blind and in pain."

"So you and Grace decided that . . ." I let the question hang.

"That she'd end her life. It's all right, Allie, it has a name — assisted suicide."

"That's so . . . extreme," Kerry says. "And it's still illegal even for physicians in most states."

Delia shrugs. "We knew all that. It's a chance we decided to take. It was what Grace wanted — some control over her death. A dignified end. It's what we all want, if we ever get the courage to look at death squarely. Grace was a very courageous woman. She supplied the will. We just helped her figure out the way."

My mouth is so dry I can hardly ask the question. "We?"

"Our friends." Delia looks over at me. "Robin and Paula. Mary and Whitney. We researched and discussed and constructed scenarios and tore them apart and constructed others. Eventually we decided on . . . what we did. Funny — it was Grace's original suggestion. Death by water, she called it. After Eliot's poem."

"Paula and Robin and the others — I saw you with them in the coffeehouse in Windsock Sunday

191

afternoon. You didn't see me," I say, grimacing. "I was behind a newspaper. You talked about . . . doing something that evening. About it being the last thing."

She nods.

"What were you doing?"

"Spreading Grace's ashes," she says. "There were . . . several spots that were special to her."

"Your friends — did they go with you to the watersports store?" I ask.

I can see that she's surprised I have this piece of information but she answers right away. "Yes they went with me."

"The fins. Why did you buy the fins?" Kerry asks.

Delia grimaces. "To snorkel."

I'm shocked. "You were the snorkeler?"

"Yes. No one but me knew how much Grace feared the water. She announced that she was taking up the sport but we figured that wasn't enough. We needed to establish the fact that she snorkeled. So I put the damned gear on and splashed around out there."

"The day . . . the day Grace died," Kerry asks, a bloodhound to the end, "how did you get back?"

"I swam back," Delia said. "Around the far side of the rocks to the pebble beach at the north end of our property. No one ever goes there. I left some clothes and shoes in a duffel bag in the rocks and when I reached the beach I just got dressed and climbed the bank."

"Weren't you afraid that someone might see you?" I ask.

She shook her head. "I sent everyone on errands

that afternoon. I was fairly certain I'd be alone. Of course, someone might have seen me, but what would they have seen? Only Cordelia walking up the path from the north end of the property. Nothing suspicious in that."

We're all quiet for a few moments and I wonder if she'll answer my question now. Because I have to know. "Will you tell me about it now?" I ask. "How it happened?"

"Do you really want to know?" Cordelia asks, turning to me. She reaches up, putting a hand on my face, and I know it's not me she's seeing but Grace, her lover. It's all right, I decide. "I'd like to know," I say.

"Tranquilizers and cold water," she says, her voice tight. "Grace figured she could get into the water if she was doped up enough so she wasn't afraid and then, well, the cold would do the job."

I'm horrified. "What if, you know, she panicked at the last moment? Changed her mind?"

"I would have pulled her out," Delia says. "But she didn't panic. That wasn't Grace's nature. She sat on the swim platform and put on a pair of fins and a mask we bought in Seattle at the Lions Thrift Shop one day when we came from her doctor's office months ago. Then she let herself down into the water. She hung onto the swim platform for fifteen or twenty minutes, talking to me, and right to the end I thought that she *would* change her mind, but she just . . . let go. Before I could do or say anything, she had slipped beneath the surface. She didn't come up."

"So much could have gone wrong," Kerry says,

shaking her head. "The medical examiner could have taken blood samples. Someone could have come along. So many things. You're lucky."

"Lucky? Am I? If you say so." Cordelia gets up, brushing sand off her pants, wiping her hands on her thighs. "Your aunt loved you," she tells me. "She kept sending you letters and cards, although you never wrote back. But she didn't give up hope." Delia laughs a little. "She even named the garden in front of the B & B after your business. She believed you'd come one day. I'm just sorry it took her death to bring you here." She holds out her hand to me. "Allison — come on back. Come to Lavner Bay. I have things that Grace wanted me to give you. And I'd like you to talk to our friends."

I panic for a minute, wondering what it would mean if I took her hand, what I'd be committing myself to, but then I realize with an incredible sense of freedom that I don't have to make any decisions at all right now. I can just let Delia help me to my feet. Or walk me to Kerry's Toyota. Or take me all the way back to Lavner Bay where I can spend as few or as many nights as I wish.

I look past Delia to the ocean's edge where the sea lion, having completed his sun bath, is making his laborious way back into the surf. The seagulls are still standing in the river runoff, undisturbed, and I suddenly see that this bay and the place my aunt built is a safe place, a haven, a shelter. I mean, it finally dawns on me what Lavner Bay is and why Grace kept calling me here. Why did it take her death to make me listen?

"Okay," I tell Delia, and hold out my hand, letting her pull me to my feet. After all, I don't have to decide my entire future in the next five minutes, now do I? The three of us walk together to Kerry's truck.

A few of the publications of
THE NAIAD PRESS, INC.
P.O. Box 10543 • Tallahassee, Florida 32302
Phone (904) 539-5965
Toll-Free Order Number: 1-800-533-1973
Mail orders welcome. Please include 15% postage.
Write or call for our free catalog which also features an
incredible selection of lesbian videos.

DEATH AT LAVENDER BAY by Lauren Wright Douglas. 208 pp. 1st Allison O'Neil Mystery. ISBN 1-56280-085-X $10.95

YES I SAID YES I WILL by Judith McDaniel. 272 pp. Hot romance by famous author. ISBN 1-56280-138-4 10.95

FORBIDDEN FIRES by Margaret C. Anderson. Edited by Mathilda Hills. 176 pp. Famous author's "unpublished" Lesbian romance. ISBN 1-56280-123-6 21.95

SIDE TRACKS by Teresa Stores. 160 pp. Gender-bending Lesbians on the road. ISBN 1-56280-122-8 10.95

HOODED MURDER by Annette Van Dyke. 176 pp. 1st Jessie Batelle Mystery. ISBN 1-56280-134-1 10.95

WILDWOOD FLOWERS by Julia Watts. 208 pp. Hilarious and heart-warming tale of true love. ISBN 1-56280-127-9 10.95

NEVER SAY NEVER by Linda Hill. 224 pp. Rule #1: Never get involved with . . . ISBN 1-56280-126-0 10.95

THE SEARCH by Melanie McAllester. 240 pp. Exciting top cop Tenny Mendoza case. ISBN 1-56280-150-3 10.95

THE WISH LIST by Saxon Bennett. 192 pp. Romance through the years. ISBN 1-56280-125-2 10.95

FIRST IMPRESSIONS by Kate Calloway. 208 pp. P.I. Cassidy James' first case. ISBN 1-56280-133-3 10.95

OUT OF THE NIGHT by Kris Bruyer. 192 pp. Spine-tingling thriller. ISBN 1-56280-120-1 10.95

NORTHERN BLUE by Tracey Richardson. 224 pp. Police recruits Miki & Miranda — passion in the line of fire. ISBN 1-56280-118-X 10.95

LOVE'S HARVEST by Peggy J. Herring. 176 pp. by the author of *Once More With Feeling.* ISBN 1-56280-117-1 10.95

THE COLOR OF WINTER by Lisa Shapiro. 208 pp. Romantic love beyond your wildest dreams. ISBN 1-56280-116-3 10.95

FAMILY SECRETS by Laura DeHart Young. 208 pp. Enthralling
romance and suspense. ISBN 1-56280-119-8   10.95

INLAND PASSAGE by Jane Rule. 288 pp. Tales exploring conven-
tional & unconventional relationships. ISBN 0-930044-56-8   10.95

DOUBLE BLUFF by Claire McNab. 208 pp. 7th Detective Carol
Ashton Mystery. ISBN 1-56280-096-5   10.95

BAR GIRLS by Lauran Hoffman. 176 pp. See the movie, read
the book! ISBN 1-56280-115-5   10.95

THE FIRST TIME EVER edited by Barbara Grier & Christine
Cassidy. 272 pp. Love stories by Naiad Press authors.
ISBN 1-56280-086-8   14.95

MISS PETTIBONE AND MISS McGRAW by Brenda Weathers.
208 pp. A charming ghostly love story. ISBN 1-56280-151-1   10.95

CHANGES by Jackie Calhoun. 208 pp. Involved romance and
relationships. ISBN 1-56280-083-3   10.95

FAIR PLAY by Rose Beecham. 256 pp. 3rd Amanda Valentine
Mystery. ISBN 1-56280-081-7   10.95

PAXTON COURT by Diane Salvatore. 256 pp. Erotic and wickedly
funny contemporary tale about the business of learning to live
together. ISBN 1-56280-109-0   21.95

PAYBACK by Celia Cohen. 176 pp. A gripping thriller of romance,
revenge and betrayal. ISBN 1-56280-084-1   10.95

THE BEACH AFFAIR by Barbara Johnson. 224 pp. Sizzling
summer romance/mystery/intrigue. ISBN 1-56280-090-6   10.95

GETTING THERE by Robbi Sommers. 192 pp. Nobody does it
like Robbi! ISBN 1-56280-099-X   10.95

FINAL CUT by Lisa Haddock. 208 pp. 2nd Carmen Ramirez
Mystery. ISBN 1-56280-088-4   10.95

FLASHPOINT by Katherine V. Forrest. 256 pp. A Lesbian
blockbuster! ISBN 1-56280-079-5   10.95

CLAIRE OF THE MOON by Nicole Conn. Audio Book —Read
by Marianne Hyatt. ISBN 1-56280-113-9   16.95

FOR LOVE AND FOR LIFE: INTIMATE PORTRAITS OF
LESBIAN COUPLES by Susan Johnson. 224 pp.
ISBN 1-56280-091-4   14.95

DEVOTION by Mindy Kaplan. 192 pp. See the movie — read
the book! ISBN 1-56280-093-0   10.95

SOMEONE TO WATCH by Jaye Maiman. 272 pp. 4th Robin
Miller Mystery. ISBN 1-56280-095-7   10.95

GREENER THAN GRASS by Jennifer Fulton. 208 pp. A young
woman — a stranger in her bed. ISBN 1-56280-092-2   10.95

TRAVELS WITH DIANA HUNTER by Regine Sands. Erotic
lesbian romp. Audio Book (2 cassettes)   ISBN 1-56280-107-4   16.95

CABIN FEVER by Carol Schmidt. 256 pp. Sizzling suspense
and passion.   ISBN 1-56280-089-1   10.95

THERE WILL BE NO GOODBYES by Laura DeHart Young. 192
pp. Romantic love, strength, and friendship.   ISBN 1-56280-103-1   10.95

FAULTLINE by Sheila Ortiz Taylor. 144 pp. Joyous comic
lesbian novel.   ISBN 1-56280-108-2   9.95

OPEN HOUSE by Pat Welch. 176 pp. 4th Helen Black Mystery.
     ISBN 1-56280-102-3   10.95

ONCE MORE WITH FEELING by Peggy J. Herring. 240 pp.
Lighthearted, loving romantic adventure.   ISBN 1-56280-089-2   10.95

FOREVER by Evelyn Kennedy. 224 pp. Passionate romance — love
overcoming all obstacles.   ISBN 1-56280-094-9   10.95

WHISPERS by Kris Bruyer. 176 pp. Romantic ghost story
     ISBN 1-56280-082-5   10.95

NIGHT SONGS by Penny Mickelbury. 224 pp. 2nd Gianna Maglione
Mystery.   ISBN 1-56280-097-3   10.95

GETTING TO THE POINT by Teresa Stores. 256 pp. Classic
southern Lesbian novel.   ISBN 1-56280-100-7   10.95

PAINTED MOON by Karin Kallmaker. 224 pp. Delicious
Kallmaker romance.   ISBN 1-56280-075-2   10.95

THE MYSTERIOUS NAIAD edited by Katherine V. Forrest &
Barbara Grier. 320 pp. Love stories by Naiad Press authors.
     ISBN 1-56280-074-4   14.95

DAUGHTERS OF A CORAL DAWN by Katherine V. Forrest.
240 pp. Tenth Anniversay Edition.   ISBN 1-56280-104-X   10.95

BODY GUARD by Claire McNab. 208 pp. 6th Carol Ashton
Mystery.   ISBN 1-56280-073-6   10.95

CACTUS LOVE by Lee Lynch. 192 pp. Stories by the beloved
storyteller.   ISBN 1-56280-071-X   9.95

SECOND GUESS by Rose Beecham. 216 pp. 2nd Amanda Valentine
Mystery.   ISBN 1-56280-069-8   9.95

THE SURE THING by Melissa Hartman. 208 pp. L.A. earthquake
romance.   ISBN 1-56280-078-7   9.95

A RAGE OF MAIDENS by Lauren Wright Douglas. 240 pp. 6th Caitlin
Reece Mystery.   ISBN 1-56280-068-X   10.95

TRIPLE EXPOSURE by Jackie Calhoun. 224 pp. Romantic drama
involving many characters.   ISBN 1-56280-067-1   10.95

UP, UP AND AWAY by Catherine Ennis. 192 pp. Delightful
romance.   ISBN 1-56280-065-5   9.95

PERSONAL ADS by Robbi Sommers. 176 pp. Sizzling short
stories.   ISBN 1-56280-059-0   10.95

FLASHPOINT by Katherine V. Forrest. 256 pp. Lesbian
blockbuster!   ISBN 1-56280-043-4   22.95

CROSSWORDS by Penny Sumner. 256 pp. 2nd Victoria Cross
Mystery.   ISBN 1-56280-064-7   9.95

SWEET CHERRY WINE by Carol Schmidt. 224 pp. A novel of
suspense.   ISBN 1-56280-063-9   9.95

CERTAIN SMILES by Dorothy Tell. 160 pp. Erotic short stories.
                                            ISBN 1-56280-066-3   9.95

EDITED OUT by Lisa Haddock. 224 pp. 1st Carmen Ramirez
Mystery.   ISBN 1-56280-077-9   9.95

WEDNESDAY NIGHTS by Camarin Grae. 288 pp. Sexy
adventure.   ISBN 1-56280-060-4   10.95

SMOKEY O by Celia Cohen. 176 pp. Relationships on the
playing field.   ISBN 1-56280-057-4   9.95

KATHLEEN O'DONALD by Penny Hayes. 256 pp. Rose and
Kathleen find each other and employment in 1909 NYC.
                                            ISBN 1-56280-070-1   9.95

STAYING HOME by Elisabeth Nonas. 256 pp. Molly and Alix
want a baby . . . or do they?   ISBN 1-56280-076-0   10.95

TRUE LOVE by Jennifer Fulton. 240 pp. Six lesbians searching
for love in all the "right" places.   ISBN 1-56280-035-3   10.95

GARDENIAS WHERE THERE ARE NONE by Molleen Zanger.
176 pp. Why is Melanie inextricably drawn to the old house?
                                            ISBN 1-56280-056-6   9.95

KEEPING SECRETS by Penny Mickelbury. 208 pp. 1st Gianna
Maglione Mystery.   ISBN 1-56280-052-3   9.95

THE ROMANTIC NAIAD edited by Katherine V. Forrest &
Barbara Grier. 336 pp. Love stories by Naiad Press authors.
                                            ISBN 1-56280-054-X   14.95

UNDER MY SKIN by Jaye Maiman. 336 pp. 3rd Robin Miller
Mystery.   ISBN 1-56280-049-3.   10.95

STAY TOONED by Rhonda Dicksion. 144 pp. Cartoons — 1st
collection since *Lesbian Survival Manual*.   ISBN 1-56280-045-0   9.95

CAR POOL by Karin Kallmaker. 272pp. Lesbians on wheels
and then some!   ISBN 1-56280-048-5   10.95

NOT TELLING MOTHER: STORIES FROM A LIFE by Diane
Salvatore. 176 pp. Her 3rd novel.   ISBN 1-56280-044-2   9.95

GOBLIN MARKET by Lauren Wright Douglas. 240pp. 5th Caitlin
Reece Mystery.   ISBN 1-56280-047-7   10.95

LONG GOODBYES by Nikki Baker. 256 pp. 3rd Virginia Kelly
Mystery. ISBN 1-56280-042-6 9.95

FRIENDS AND LOVERS by Jackie Calhoun. 224 pp. Mid-
western Lesbian lives and loves. ISBN 1-56280-041-8 10.95

THE CAT CAME BACK by Hilary Mullins. 208 pp. Highly
praised Lesbian novel. ISBN 1-56280-040-X 9.95

BEHIND CLOSED DOORS by Robbi Sommers. 192 pp. Hot,
erotic short stories. ISBN 1-56280-039-6 9.95

CLAIRE OF THE MOON by Nicole Conn. 192 pp. See the
movie — read the book! ISBN 1-56280-038-8 10.95

SILENT HEART by Claire McNab. 192 pp. Exotic Lesbian
romance. ISBN 1-56280-036-1 10.95

HAPPY ENDINGS by Kate Brandt. 272 pp. Intimate conversations
with Lesbian authors. ISBN 1-56280-050-7 10.95

THE SPY IN QUESTION by Amanda Kyle Williams. 256 pp.
4th Madison McGuire Mystery. ISBN 1-56280-037-X 9.95

SAVING GRACE by Jennifer Fulton. 240 pp. Adventure and
romantic entanglement. ISBN 1-56280-051-5 9.95

THE YEAR SEVEN by Molleen Zanger. 208 pp. Women surviving
in a new world. ISBN 1-56280-034-5 9.95

CURIOUS WINE by Katherine V. Forrest. 176 pp. Tenth Anniver-
sary Edition. The most popular contemporary Lesbian love story.
ISBN 1-56280-053-1 10.95
Audio Book (2 cassettes) ISBN 1-56280-105-8 16.95

CHAUTAUQUA by Catherine Ennis. 192 pp. Exciting, romantic
adventure. ISBN 1-56280-032-9 9.95

A PROPER BURIAL by Pat Welch. 192 pp. 3rd Helen Black
Mystery. ISBN 1-56280-033-7 9.95

SILVERLAKE HEAT: A Novel of Suspense by Carol Schmidt.
240 pp. Rhonda is as hot as Laney's dreams. ISBN 1-56280-031-0 9.95

LOVE, ZENA BETH by Diane Salvatore. 224 pp. The most talked
about lesbian novel of the nineties! ISBN 1-56280-030-2 10.95

A DOORYARD FULL OF FLOWERS by Isabel Miller. 160 pp.
Stories incl. 2 sequels to *Patience and Sarah.* ISBN 1-56280-029-9 9.95

These are just a few of the many Naiad Press titles — we are the oldest and
largest lesbian/feminist publishing company in the world. We also offer an
enormous selection of lesbian video products. Please request a complete
catalog. We offer personal service; we encourage and welcome direct mail
orders from individuals who have limited access to bookstores carrying our
publications.